DARLENE P. CAMPOS

Heaven Isn't Me

Contents

Chapter 1

Everyone in my neighborhood has a nickname except me. Most of the nicknames are freaking ridiculous, but it makes me wonder why I don't have something everyone else has. Mom named me. She wanted something that sounded heavenly. She thought of "Celestial," "Estrella," and "Paradise." Dad, the most scientific minded person ever, came up with "Cloud." Hardly anyone can pronounce my name, especially the rest of my family.

"Elsa!"

"Ella!"

"Eliza!"

"Elsy!"

"East!"

You could say those are nicknames, but they're not – they're words my family calls me because they can't say my name correctly. Or, maybe they can and they don't care. They probably don't care.

When Mom and Dad left for Buenos Aires, I thought I was dying. My aunt, whose nickname is Sazón, was home with me. She sat back on the couch, squinting her eyes and licking her lips. My breathing quickened, my heart jumped, sweat built up from my forehead and rushed down my face.

"What the heck are you doing?" she asked.

"I don't know, it's just happening," I said through harder breaths.

"Well, stop it."

"I can't."

"Yeah you can," she said, swinging her big hand onto my back. "You can do anything you put your mind to, right?"

"Not for this, Aunt Sazón."

"You're just worried about your parents," she said with a long sigh. "They'll be back before Christmas. You're a big girl anyway, you don't need them as much anymore."

She was right, but whatever was happening to me didn't let me keep that thought in my head. I kept thinking about Mom and Dad in ways I couldn't understand. I kept thinking *what if their plane crashes? What if they get kidnapped? What if the school where they're teaching doesn't like them? What if they like Buenos Aires so much, they never come home? What if they like it so much, they make me move away with them? What if the school steals their passports, holds them hostage, and they never come home again? What if they die and my new parents are Aunt Sazón and Uncle Pico? Or Uncle Juke? More like Uncle Puke.*

"Elly, stop it!" Aunt Sazón said. "You're shaking like it's cold in here!"

I breathed in slowly, held the air in my body gently, and then breathed out. Mom and Dad traveled for work a lot. Sometimes they took me along if school was out, but if school was in, I stayed home. Mom and Dad had gone all the way to South Korea, Australia, and New Zealand before. Buenos Aires was far from Rey Carlos Island, but it wasn't as far as New Zealand. Why was I worried?

"You done yet?" Aunt Sazón asked, her eyes rolling.

"I think so," I said. My mind wasn't racing with questions anymore and my heart finally slowed down along with my breathing.

"This ever happened before?" she asked.

"I can't remember," I answered, trying to think back, but no memories came to me. "I guess I miss my parents. No biggie."

"They've gone away tons of times before, Elly."

I scrunched up my nose and took a big gulp. "That's not my name."

"Whatever. You think my name is actually Sazón?"

"It's Katarina."

"Yeah, but nobody calls me Katarina and I don't care. What do you want for dinner?"

"I'm eating at Lalo's tonight," I said.

Her eyes rolled again, like I said I was going to eat dinner with drug lords. "Boys, boys, boys. You need to be careful with them."

"You have three sons," I reminded her. If anyone needed to watch out for dumb boys, it was for her three sons.

"Mine are different," she said. Yes, they were. Different in an extremely bad way.

At five, I walked down the street to Lalo's house. His real name is Eduardo Carlos Richardson, but like the rest of our neighborhood, he has a nickname. We met in kindergarten, when I pushed him out of my way in the ice cream line at the school cafeteria. We sat out during recess because he tried to push me back and our teacher saw him. While we sat together, we weren't supposed to talk, but we did.

"Do you push EVERYONE?" he said, sweating from the heavy Texas heat.

"Anyone who's in my way," I said, waving my fist at him.

"That's not nice."

"I'm not nice!"

"But nice is good!"

"But nice is *gooooood*," I said, mocking his voice. Then he started crying and told me I was a meanie butt. We had been best friends ever since.

"What took you so long?" Lalo asked when he let me inside his house.

"Sorry, I was pushing everyone I saw in the neighborhood!"

"Even the old ladies?"

"Especially the old ladies!"

"Elysian! Don't do that. The old ladies who live here are nice."

"Of course, I won't *actually* do that, Lalo," I said. "What's for dinner?"

"Uh, I'm not sure," he said, scratching his head. "It's something."

"Is it gross?"

"No, it smells good," he said. "I just don't know what it is." I followed him to the kitchen where he pulled a lid off a pot. We looked inside and saw bell pepper chunks, broccoli florets, black beans, and some kind of meat or meat substitute that Lalo's parents ate sometimes. Mrs. Richardson's nickname is Mrs. Feelgood. She's a nightshift nurse at Southern Texas Hospital. Mr. Richardson runs his own A/C company under his nickname, Big Chilly's Cold Air.

"At least it smells good," I said.

"I hope it's not squid."

"Squid? Why would your parents want to eat squid?"

"They like weird stuff. Here, take a plate and get however much you want."

I ate with Lalo in front of his gigantic TV. We watched an easy trivia show, but the three contestants were getting every single answer wrong. Since we couldn't take their stupidity anymore, we switched the channel to another show where the featured people wanted to buy a house and their budgets were like ten million dollars.

"With that much money, you can buy a bunch of houses," Lalo said. "There should be a show where people have to buy a week's worth of groceries with fifty bucks. That's way more impressive."

"Who wants to see people shop for food?" I asked.

"Hey! I'd watch it!"

"You'd watch a show about dirt farmers."

"Dirt farmers?" he said. "There are farmers who farm dirt?"

"Change the channel. These people are getting on my nerves."

Lalo grabbed the remote and switched the channel to a documentary about the history of pizza. It was interesting, but I daydreamed within a few minutes and lost track. I thought about Mom and Dad and how I hadn't eaten a homemade meal in forever. Mom and Dad hardly ever cooked since they were always either teaching at the University of Saint Jerome, grading their students' work or writing textbooks. Since they were always busy, they either bought fast food or we ate cereal for dinner.

"Hello! Elysian!" Lalo said, clapping his hands in my face. "You dozed off again!"

"What are they talking about now? Pepperoni?"

"I don't know, I dozed off, too," he said. "Your stupid aunt called and said it's time to go home. You better go, I don't wanna get in trouble."

"You won't get in trouble, you're a boy."

"So?"

"She doesn't care about what boys do, just girls. That's why she's super nosy with me. She thinks girls are dumb."

"The only one who's dumb is her."

"Yeah, I bet her brain is made out of rocks."

I got up from the floor and walked towards the door. The phone rang and Lalo rushed to answer. It was his older sister, Gladys. Her nickname was Glad Bag, but she stopped going by that as soon as she left the neighborhood.

"Hi Gladys!" I said loud enough for her to hear me.

"Hey Elysian!" I heard her say.

"She's going home before her dumb aunt calls the cops," Lalo said, waving to me. I walked outside, already sweaty by the time I made it to the next house. While I walked, I counted my steps. When that got boring, I counted each car that drove past me. By the time I got home, Aunt Sazón was there in her bright, flamingo-pink pajamas with her hair in a big bun.

"Time for bed!" she announced.

"It's barely after seven."

"Girls your age need beauty sleep."

"And some of us need more beauty sleep than others," I whispered to myself.

"What?"

"Nothing."

"If you're not sleepy, change into your pajamas and lie in bed with your eyes closed. You'll fall asleep in minutes."

"I don't have pajamas," I said.

"Girls need pajamas."

"You're right, how can girls be girls if they don't have pajamas?"

I walked off to my bedroom where the temperature was always freezing, thanks to the ceiling's three vents. When I was younger, my bedroom used to be at the end of the hallway and Mom and Dad used my current bedroom as their home office. They purposely wanted the room cold, so they could stay awake to keep working throughout the night. But when they decided I needed a bigger bedroom, we switched. The bedroom had built-in bookcases, shelves, a digital fireplace, and hardwood flooring. Compared to my old room, it was a palace. I changed into my sleeping clothes: an old black t-shirt and blue mesh shorts. I lied in bed for a while, but my eyes stayed open. For the last couple of nights, my sleep schedule had been totally off. The weirdest thing was I felt tired a lot, yet every time I tried to sleep, I couldn't.

"Are you in bed, Ella?" Aunt Sazón said from behind my bedroom door. I made snoring sounds and heard her walk away. By the time I fell asleep, it was three in the morning.

Chapter 2

At school the next day, I struggled to keep my eyes open. My first class of the day was Geology with Mr. Garrison. He was nice, but there's not really an exciting way to teach about rocks.

"Class, now when the sand, shells, and pebbles join together, they create sediment, known as sedimentary rock," he said, slower than a tired turtle. "And that's when things really start to get exciting."

"This guy is such a loser," my friend Brandon whispered to me. He didn't have a nickname, but he also didn't live in my neighborhood. He lived across the street in Westmill Park with his dad, Mr. Isaac Meyer. He was the head bouncer at Isle of Darkness, a nightclub in downtown Rey Carlos.

"Every person has a special interest," I told him.

"They're freaking rocks."

"Someone's gotta study them."

"Why? Not like rocks can cure cancer," he said.

"For extra credit," Mr. Garrison said when the bell was about to ring. "Go to the beach this weekend and see if you can find sedimentary rocks. Bring a few to class for five extra points on your final exam at the end of the semester."

The bell rang and I scrammed out of the classroom with

Brandon by my side, tugging at his shirt like he always did when he walked.

"Boy, I can't wait until high school," he said. "One more year of this junkyard."

"This place?" I said. "This is nothing. This is a good school. Try Hemlock."

"I still don't get why anyone would name a school after a poisonous plant. That's like getting a cute puppy and naming it Charlie Manson."

We had different classes next, so we walked in opposite directions when we got to the second floor. Madrazo Middle School was three stories high, but it was narrow. Before it became a school, the building was an abandoned children's hospital from the 1960s. The hallways were long and tight, the classrooms still looked like labs, and there were vending machines where the elevators used to be. When Lalo and I were in third grade, we snuck into the old hospital. It was neat to see everything left behind like beds, wheelchairs, clipboards, and medicine bottles. There were tons of old stuffed animals, too. It was creepy, but interesting. We enjoyed looking around until a pack of rats ran past and scared the hell out of us. When we were in fourth grade, the Rey Carlos School District bought the building and restored it into Madrazo Middle School since Nimitz and Hemlock were overcrowded. Lalo and me missed the old hospital, but it was kind of neat to go to school in it.

When I got to math class, I tried to complete the worksheet Ms. Bautista gave us. We weren't allowed to use a calculator either. Lalo was in math with me, which meant absolutely nothing, because numbers confused him way more than they did me.

"Hey!" he said, leaning himself towards my desk. "What the heck is this stuff?"

"Math."

"I mean, how do I start?" he asked.

"No idea."

"Huh? But you're smart."

"Not for math," I said.

"Whatever," Lalo said. "I'll just flunk," He scribbled his name on his worksheet, got up, and turned it in totally blank. Ms. Bautista gave credit for everything. Writing your name on your worksheet was worth 15 points. She probably gave out points for breathing in class. In the rest of my classes, an F was anything below a 60 average. In Ms. Bautista's class, an F was anything below a 30. The math was hard, but at least it was hard to fail.

"Do you know what your average is?" I asked Lalo when he got back to his desk.

"I dunno. I hope it's a 31."

"Last time I checked, I had an 80," I said.

"80? And you're worried about not understanding the new stuff we learn? Who cares? Come join The 31 Club with me."

I rolled my eyes and sighed. I always wished Lalo took school a little more seriously. I was better at school work, but he was smarter than me in a lot of other ways. Lalo knew how to change a flat tire, catch fish, make a bird house from loose wood pieces, find his way around in new places, and convince stray animals to approach him, so he could feed them. He was bloated with knowledge, but school wasn't for him.

When the bell rang again, it was lunchtime. I walked with Lalo down the hallway and then we pushed our way through the crowd to get to the main stairwell. As we eased ourselves down the huge, sticky steps, my heart raced. I called out to Lalo, but he couldn't hear me over everyone else trying to get downstairs. There were other kids talking loudly, Principal Jarmon and Vice

Principal Reismann yelled at everyone to move along quickly, and there was static from the intercom on the ceiling. By the time I walked in the cafeteria, I needed a breather and chose the table closest to the entrance. Lalo sat next to me, chewing and gulping down the leftovers from last night's mystery dinner.

"What are you doing?" I asked.

"Eating."

"Why are you eating so loud?"

"What?"

"The way you eat is super loud. Tone it down."

"Uh, okay?" he said, pausing and patting the sides of his mouth with his napkin.

"I didn't say you *couldn't* eat, I just said you're eating way too loud."

"Elysian, what the hell, dude? Are you mad at me?"

"No," I said, but I was confused on what I was feeling. I looked at his face, his little eyes looking back at me. He was cute when he wasn't eating.

"What's up?" he asked. "I'll quiet down if you need me to."

"It's fine," I said, sighing. "I'm fine."

"You don't look fine."

"What are you trying to say?" I asked sharply.

"Nothing," he said, clearing his throat. "It's just, I don't know. You're different whenever your parents travel."

"I am?"

"Yeah," he said. Brandon sat down finally, chewing on a hot chicken taco he got from the snack line. The smell of the spices flew to my nose and made me cough a few times.

"Whoa, what am I missing?" Brandon asked.

"Lalo hates me," I said as a joke. But within seconds, my mind raced and I thought *what if Lalo does hate me? What if we're only friends because we're both dorks? What if we're friends because his parents pay him to be friends with me? No, they wouldn't pay him anything, they're too cheap, Lalo's allowance is only five bucks a week.*

"Elysian," Brandon said, snapping his fingers in my face. "You all right?"

"What happened?" I asked.

"You just said I hated you," Lalo said. "That's not true. I hate math!"

"I was kidding, I know you don't hate me," I said, still unsure. "Hey Brandon, do I change when my parents travel? Lalo said I do."

"Sure," Brandon agreed. "You get angrier because you have to deal with your aunt and your weird uncles."

"Hmm," I said. "Yeah, you're right."

"Don't worry," Brandon said, swallowing the last bit of his greasy taco. "Moods change like the weather. You're still you."

But I wasn't. I hadn't been me in a while.

Chapter 3

On Saturday, I headed to Emerald Beach with Lalo and Brandon to find sedimentary rocks. Tiana joined us too. She was in Mr. Garrison's afternoon geology class with Lalo. I didn't know her very well, but she tagged along with me, Lalo, and Brandon whenever she could.

"Oh boy, rocks!" she said as we walked down Ocean Avenue. "This is gonna be fun!"

"We're only doing this crap for the extra credit," Brandon said.

"You mean you don't like geology?" Tiana asked, her green eyes fluttering at Brandon like he was steak.

"Nope," he said. "Hate it."

"It's easier than math," Lalo said. "It's rocks."

"Like the ones you got in your head," I said.

"Shut up, Elysian," Lalo answered. "Go push people."

The walk to Emerald Beach took longer than usual since most of the sidewalks were closed off for construction. We walked along Seaside Boulevard, stuck behind tons of tourists because most of the souvenir shops were on that street. The USS Defiance, a warship docked on Emerald Beach ever since 1946, was in the distance. It was a museum and though I hardly went to it, I found myself wanting to, so I didn't have to listen to Tiana drool over Brandon.

"Gladys is here today, somewhere," Lalo said when we got to Emerald Beach at last. "She's doing a modeling session. She told me about it earlier this week."

"Your sister's a model?" Tiana said. "That's so cool!"

"Instagram model," Lalo said. "And she's not super famous, yet. She does it to make extra money. Some magazine photographer from Austin is interested in her."

"Of course, man," Brandon said. "Your sister's hot."

"Shut up!" Lalo said.

"What? If she wasn't hot, she wouldn't be an Instagram model," Brandon answered.

"She's not hot," Lalo said, gagging. "She's my big sister for God's sake. She used to change my diapers."

"Doesn't make her any less hot," Brandon said, shrugging his shoulders.

"Enough," I butted in. "We need to find these stupid rocks."

We walked around the beach for an hour before we found any solid rocks. They were hard and smelled like ocean water. I grabbed three for myself and Brandon, Tiana, and Lalo grabbed two each. Then I grabbed more in case I lost mine. After we had our rocks packed in a bag, we chilled out by the water. We mostly sat on the sand, but when the sun was extra heavy, putting our feet in the water helped us cool down.

"It's hot, man. Hotter than Gladys. Right, Lalo?" Brandon asked, rubbing sweat off his face with his hands. "What the hell is up with this weather?" He pulled his giant wallet out of his back pocket and placed it on his stomach. He never carried much money, but it weighed as much as a rock and was stuffed with photos of his grandparents, current and expired coupons, reward cards, folded napkins and a beat-up laminated card with his phone number, address, blood type, date of birth, and a list of his allergies.

"You need to wear sunscreen," Lalo told him. "You're burning up like a campfire. I could make s'mores on you."

"Oh, Brandon," Tiana said in her bubbly voice, with her eyeballs dancing. "You don't need to do anything except be yourself."

"You know what? I'm gonna get ice cream from Jasper's," Brandon said. "I got all of you. What flavors do y'all want?"

"Chocolate," Lalo said immediately.

"Ooooh, I'll take coffee," Tiana said, licking her upper lip.

"None for me," I said. "Thanks though."

"Are you sure, Elysian?" Brandon asked. "It's hotter than the devil's asshole out here."

"I'm okay. Really."

"Can I get the ice cream with you, Brandon?" Tiana asked, already standing up.

"Sure," he answered. "Lalo?"

"Yeah, I'm coming," Lalo said. "You wanna save our spot, Elysian?"

"I'll be here," I said.

The three of them walked away and I lied down on the hot sand. Eventually, the sand got too hot, so I sat up to cool my back off. I squinted my eyes and saw Lalo, Brandon, and Tiana standing in line for ice cream by the other beach stands.

Sammy's Shades sold crappy sunglasses, Unique Umbrellas were not unique at all, and Koala Towels had towels so thin, they were wrecked after two or three washes. Jasper's Ice Cream always had a long line. Two years back, when Rey Carlos Island went through Hurricane Sally, Mr. Jasper was on the evening news screaming "STILL OPEN FOR BUSINESS!" until a giant wave came behind him and he ran out of the camera's shot along with the journalist. As I watched my buddies and Tiana wait in line, I noticed a black SUV driving by the beach stands. When it got to the end of the block, it made a quick U-turn and returned to the stands. It parked, but the beach parking lots were further down from the stands. Something seemed off, but everything had seemed off to me lately.

"He's got a gun!" I heard someone scream. The gunshots were so loud, they were all I could hear, even after they stopped. I crawled away slowly and lied still on the sand in silence until a police officer asked me to stand up.

Chapter 4

I sat in the ER waiting room with Aunt Sazón, Uncle Pico, and Uncle Juke at Southern Texas Hospital. Tiana was shot in her hip, Lalo was grazed on his elbow, and Brandon was shot in his butt, but luckily for him, most of the bullet got lodged in his wallet. There were two types of people at the ER waiting room: those who were calm and those were sobbing enough to create puddles on the cold floor. For some reason, I was the first type. Aunt Sazón tapped Uncle Pico on his shoulder to get his attention. He and Uncle Juke were focused on the Cowboys game on the television even though they were losing miserably.

"Pico!" she said. "I'm talking!"

"Yes, love?" Uncle Pico said.

"I said what do you want from the cafeteria?"

"Cafeteria? I want homemade food."

"I can't cook today, we could be here for hours! We have to stay until Lalo gets out, so we can take him home," Aunt Sazón said.

"Kid can walk, he just got grazed," Uncle Pico said, yawning.

"Yeah, I got shot when I was in the Damned Dynamites," Uncle Juke said. "Chest, center, barely missed my heart. Ain't too bad."

"Uncle Juke, you were thirty. Lalo is thirteen," I said, but he ranted about how Lalo needed to be a man. He barely knew Lalo to begin with, yet every single time he talked about him, he always complained about how unmanly Lalo was because he was close to Gladys.

"A man should be out working, getting sweaty, picking up chicks," he said near the end of his magnificent lecture. "Not calling his sister like a sissy."

"I think it's sweet," I said.

"Of course you do," Uncle Juke said. "You're the only one who always thinks the opposite of everything that's normal."

"I'm outta here," I said. Aunt Sazón told me to hold on, but I didn't. The second I stepped outside, the sun warmed my freezing skin. Cop cars and news vans were all over the main entrance of the hospital. I looked ahead and walked quickly, avoiding the cameras the best I could. I didn't know what I would say to a journalist. *Would I say I thought something was up with the SUV? That I stayed flat on the sand like a piece of trash while my friends bled?*

I found a desolate courtyard with fake trees, wooden tables, and a fountain with green water and sat for a minute to breathe. I breathed in, out, in, out for a long time. I'm not sure how long I stayed outside, but by the time I was ready to go back inside the ER waiting room, my clothes were drenched in sweat.

"Look at you," Uncle Pico said when I sat by him. "Did you go swimming?"

"No, I took a walk."

"A walk? In this heat?"

"Sure, why not?"

"A nice girl like you shouldn't sweat," he said, putting his feet up on the chair across from us. "Boys don't like sweaty girls."

"I don't care what they like or don't like right now, Uncle

Pico," I said.

"Just giving you pointers," he said. "When I met your aunt, she wasn't sweaty."

"I need to use the restroom," I said, standing up. "I'll be right back. Where did Aunt Sazón and Uncle Juke go?"

"Cafeteria," Uncle Pico answered with a small burp.

I walked towards the restroom and when I saw that Uncle Pico wasn't looking, I snuck inside the ER entrance behind a tall nurse. Lalo was in Room 10, sipping on a carton of apple juice and watching *Jeopardy!*

"Hey!" he said. "Can you be in here?"

"I snuck in."

"Did you push people to get in?"

"I pushed *all* the people!" I said.

"Hah! My mom stopped by and told me I'm going home soon. Do you know if anyone died? I'm glad I'm okay, but I'm worried about everyone else who was there."

"I'm not sure," I said. "I haven't paid attention to the news. Where are Tiana and Brandon?"

"No idea," Lalo said, lowering the volume on the TV with his bedside remote. "We're fine though. Don't worry about us."

"Dude! All of you got shot!"

"I was grazed!"

"Lalo!"

"Grazed, Elysian, grazed," he said. "You better get out of here before you get caught. These nurses are vicious."

"You want me to sit in the waiting room with my aunt and my uncles?"

"Oh man. Getting grazed is better!"

I rushed out of the ER before anyone saw me. Aunt Sazón and Uncle Pico ate greasy shrimp and rice with strong slurps. Uncle

Juke loudly munched on a giant burrito. Aunt Sazón asked me if I wanted anything to eat, but I didn't. Instead, I rested my head against the wall behind me. By the time I woke up, it was nighttime. I was still in the cold waiting room, covered in thick sweat.

Chapter 5

School was different without Lalo and Brandon. They needed to stay home and rest for a week. Tiana did, too. After school was out on Monday, I walked to Tiana's house, which wasn't far from my neighborhood. Her parents owned a bakery on 5th Street called Pastry Pete's. They made good sweets, especially cakes. The roof sagged, the front door looked like it was going to come off the hinges any second and the grass was almost as tall as the house. The fence was slowly coming apart, post by post. Their bakery was small, but always full of business. I rang the doorbell and Tiana quickly came to the door.

"Elysian!"

"Hey."

She grabbed me by my arm and shoved me inside her house. We sat in her living room, on a worn-out couch, next to a black and white television set. It was 2018—what the hell kind of house was this?

"Thanks for coming by!" she said. "My parents practically live at the bakery, so I usually have the house to myself. How was school?"

"Garrison gave us those bonus points. He didn't ask to see the rocks. He knew we went to the beach because of the news."

"Aw, that's sweet! Have you heard from Brandon and Lalo?"

"Yeah, they're doing well," I said, wishing the conversation would end soon. "I wanted to make sure you were okay, too."

"Oh, I'm fine. I can't believe no one died! Either we got lucky or the shooter was lousy. I'm happy you're okay! Staying on the sand was a great idea."

"Someone needed to save our spot."

"I should've stayed behind with you," she said. "I didn't need to go with Lalo and Brandon. We could've had girl talk!"

"Oh my God," I said, which I didn't mean to say out loud. I excused myself to her bathroom. Like the rest of the house, it looked horrible. The toilet had a delicate lace cover, that was tacky as hell and made it look like the toilet was on its way to a quinceañera. The paint on the walls was peeled off, the mirror was cracked, and the sink was stained with coffee. I didn't need to use the bathroom, but I flushed the fancy toilet a couple times to make Tiana think I was sick. I threw in retching sounds for special effect.

She knocked on the bathroom door. "Are you okay?"

"I'm okay," I said. "Don't mind me. Your toilet is pretty."

"Thanks, I picked out the cover myself! Do you want tea? Tea helps me when my stomach hurts."

"Yeah, I'll take some."

I heard her footsteps get further away, which gave me the chance to relax for a minute. Tiana was nice. She was actually *very* nice. But for whatever reason, everything about her was irritating. Her voice, her gestures, her eyes, her lip licking. I didn't know if the problem was me or her. She had never done anything wrong to me—she just annoyed me. We were sort of friends, I guess, but not close friends for sure. When I felt stable enough to face her again, I came out of the bathroom. I heard water boiling and her humming the tune of "Shave and a Haircut." Since her house was cramped, the kitchen was easy to find.

"Did you puke everything out?"

"Tons," I said, holding my stomach.

"Your tea's almost ready."

"Thanks," I said, sitting at her kitchen table. Cow stickers were on the cabinets, refrigerator, stove, toaster, and blender. When the water boiled, she shut the burner off and dipped two bags of tea into the pot. While she waited for the tea to take over the hot water, she served me a plate of chips and salsa. I couldn't believe it. She had been shot in her hip days ago, but here she was waiting on me. Maybe I was the problem.

"You need to get something back in your stomach," she said. "When I was at the hospital, I didn't want to eat anything. I lost my appetite."

"I've lost my appetite, too. Before, I would get hungry all the time, and now, I can barely finish a snack. It's been going on for like three or four months."

"Oh," Tiana said as she carefully ladled tea into a mug. "That doesn't sound normal. Everyone should get hungry."

Everyone got hungry at least once a day. Or at least they're supposed to. Getting hungry is normal, so not having an appetite was one more thing to add to my abnormal list.

"Thanks for the tea," I said. "It's good."

"Yeah, it is," she said, nodding like she had turned into a bobblehead. "Tea is awesome. It tastes amazing and it doesn't have calories."

"Huh?"

"You know, calories," she repeated. "Those stupid things that make you fat."

"Everyone needs to eat to live," I said, though I was barely eating.

"Oh, Eh-lee-shun," she said, pronouncing my name incorrectly. "Boys like thin girls, especially high school boys."

"Really?" I said. "You mean if we make sure we're thin, we'll get a boy who solely likes us for our weight? Oh boy!"

"You're a smart ass," Tiana told me, clicking her tongue on the right side of her mouth. "You might think it's dumb, but it's true."

The moment I finished my tea, I made up an excuse to leave. I said I was going to help Aunt Sazón cook, but if Tiana knew me well, she'd know toast and cereal were my gourmet fixings. She walked me outside, hugged me, and thanked me for coming by. She waddled herself back to her house, saying she'd see me soon. Instead of going home, I walked to Lalo's. Brandon was there, too. They were watching a rerun of *Jerry Springer* and sharing a big bag of sour cream and onion chips.

"Y'all got shot, your lives flashed in front of your eyes, you're happy to be alive and could be doing anything, yet y'all chose to watch Springer?" I asked, sitting on the floor by them.

"This one's good," Lalo said, offering me chips. "That lady is sleeping with her cousin and her aunt found out. But it turns out they're all sleeping together."

"That's disgusting!" I said.

"Hell yeah it is," Brandon agreed. "This is stuff you'd see at my family reunion."

"Brandon, your family isn't anywhere near anything on Springer," Lalo said. "One of my uncles gets naked and chases people in his neighborhood."

"What? Who's that?" I asked.

"Uncle Kirk. He lives in Austin," he said. "What are you doing here anyway, Elysian? Doesn't your aunt want you home?"

"Probably."

"Has she called you?"

"Twice while I walked over here."

"You better get home," Brandon said.

"I don't want to," I said.

"If you don't, she'll come here," Brandon warned me. Right after he said that, the doorbell rang. Lalo got up and rushed to the door, but it wasn't Aunt Sazón.

"Are your parents home, kid?" the cop at the door asked.

"No," Lalo said in a soft voice. "I can give you their work numbers, Officer."

"Sure, write them down," the cop said, handing Lalo a water-damaged notepad. Lalo scribbled on the notepad quickly. "Thank you, young man. Be safe," the cop said, tipping his hat. Lalo shut the door, blinked quickly, and scratched at his cheeks.

"Lalo?" Brandon asked from the living room. "You doing something illegal?"

"No!" he said.

"Lalo?" I scoffed. "Lalo can't even skip class."

"I didn't do anything! Did I? Crap!" Lalo said. "All right, you guys are gonna have to be my alibi. I've been here at home with both of you watching Springer and eating chips. Got it?"

"Lalo, that's *exactly* what we've been doing," Brandon answered. "Chill."

"What if they think I did the shooting?" Lalo said, breathing heavily. "Man! All I wanted was some damn ice cream!"

"C'mon Lalo," I said, patting his left shoulder. "You were a victim. Plus, there's no way in hell you could ever shoot a gun."

"I bet I could! No, I can't," he said, shaking his head. "I wonder what that cop wanted."

"He wanted you to chill out," Brandon said, yawning. "Bro, get back in here and let's finish Springer. The family's about to beat each other up."

"I'm gonna head home," I told them. "See you guys later."

"Watch your back," Brandon reminded me. "Whoever shot up the beach is out there. Be careful, okay?"

"Yeah, Elysian," Lalo chimed in. "Don't talk to strange people."

"Too late—I already talk to you guys," I said, stepping outside. They didn't know how careful I already was. Walking anywhere meant looking around every few seconds to make sure everything was safe. Ever since the shooting, there were tons of police cars all over Rey Carlos Island. The police cars didn't make me feel safer—they made me feel like I lived in a dangerous place. As I walked home, I spotted five police cars drive past me. None of them had sirens on and none of them stopped me. But during the walk home, my heart raced. My heart raced for the rest of the day.

Chapter 6

By the time Lalo, Brandon, and Tiana were back at school, everyone knew why a cop went to Lalo's house. Gladys had been reported missing by her husband Octavio. Her last known location was Emerald Beach at the same time and the same day we were there for our rock assignment. She posted a selfie on Instagram while she waited for the magazine photographer to show up. It was timestamped 2:33 pm, ten minutes before the shooting. Lalo was a total wreck. He'd burst into tears during class and wouldn't eat at lunch.

"Where could she be?" he asked as we walked home one afternoon.

"Do you think she ran away?"

"To where?" Lalo asked again. "Houston? She ran away to sit in traffic?"

"Did she talk about going somewhere? Maybe college?" I asked.

"No," he said, his voice breaking. "Where is she, Elysian? Where did she go?"

I wished I could tell him. Gladys was extremely smart. You could ask her about any subject and she'd know something about it. She met Octavio at Rey Carlos Community College. After she graduated with a cosmetology certificate, she and Octavio moved in together and got married a year later. I remember my whole neighborhood talking about how wrong it was for her. They called her a "slut," "whore," and "easy." I didn't get why she was being name called, but not Octavio. Aunt Sazón said girls weren't supposed to move in with any man unless they were married first. But what about boys?

The last time I saw Gladys, she was helping Mrs. Richardson cook chicken and waffles for dinner. She was tall and muscular and her black hair had streaks of red, purple, and blue. I literally had to look up whenever she was around, but I looked up to her as a person, too. My parents were the highest educated people in the neighborhood and they tended to make sure everyone was aware of their superior intelligence. Gladys was different though. You could just tell how smart she was whenever she talked to you.

"Did she have any other social media accounts?" I asked Lalo. "You can see if she's posted anything recently."

"She does, but her Instagram was connected to all of them," he said. "So it's just the same selfie. There aren't any other clues."

"I wonder why we didn't see her," I said. "I know Emerald Beach is huge, but she knew you had a geology project, right?"

"She did," he said. "But I didn't want to bother her. I thought she'd be busy taking pictures. I should've bothered her."

Instead of going home like I should've, I stayed at Lalo's for an hour. We shared plain crackers for a snack and tried watching TV, but Lalo couldn't focus. He'd get up every few seconds and look around the whole living room.

"The shooting was a distraction, wasn't it?" he asked loudly, which surprised me.

"What?"

"The shooting," he said, showing me his scarred elbow.

"I don't think so, Lalo. You and a lot of other people were hurt."

"Yeah, but no one *died*. Somebody always dies in a shooting."

He had a point. I thought back to the day, trying to remember if anything else seemed off. All I could remember was the SUV, people screaming, and the pops of the bullets. I had covered my face, so there must have been a lot I didn't see.

"This shooter was probably really, really bad," I told Lalo. "And that's why no one died."

"Or," Lalo said. "The shooter was smart. He distracted an entire beach. You know how hard that is?"

"Gladys is okay," I said. In my mind, Gladys was dead or dying. *She was kidnapped and murdered, or she was hidden in someone's house where she was being tortured. Eventually, she'd die. Her kidnapper would take her body and hide her somewhere so secretive, Lalo and his family would never find out what happened to her.*

"How do you know she's okay?" he asked. "You didn't see anything."

"She's a smart woman. I'm sure she's alive."

"You promise?"

"Yeah, I do," I lied.

Lalo walked me to his door. He was tearing up, but he patted his face with his hands so I wouldn't notice. I darted down the street, hoping I could make it home before Aunt Sazón. My feet tightened as I rushed through the neighborhood. When I arrived, Uncle Pico was there, sitting on the porch swing with his legs wide open.

"You're late," he said.

"I'm not late."

"You know you're supposed to come straight home."

"Yeah, yeah."

"Ella," he said, reaching into his pocket for gum. He pulled out a stick and chewed loud enough to wake up everyone buried at LBJ Cemetery on the other side of Rey Carlos. "What's your deal with your aunt?"

"Nothing," I said. If I explained what the real deal was, he'd be sitting on the porch swing for the next twenty years.

"She thinks you don't like her."

"Not true," I said, looking up to make sure lightning wasn't about to strike me.

"You come home late. You don't listen. You do whatever you want. C'mon, girl. How are you gonna get married?"

"What does that have to do with getting married? I'm surprised you're married."

"My Lord Jesus Christ," he said, opening his eyes up fully. "What the heck is that supposed to mean, Elly?"

"Elysian!" I said. "My name is Elysian! *Eh-lee-see-un*. I can't believe Aunt Sazón would marry you, because you don't do anything for her! You're retired and you sit around all day bitching about anyone who does anything differently than you. You don't cook, you don't do dishes, you don't do any thing except *BITCH*!"

Uncle Pico stood up and slapped me across my face. For someone who didn't do anything all day, he was strong. His face was red like the bricks of my house. For a minute, I was angry at my parents. I understood they were important professors and it meant they got invited to teach at other schools, but why was their job more important than me? Whenever they took off, I had to stay on Rey Carlos Island with Aunt Stupid and Uncle Stupider and Uncle Puke.

"That's where you're wrong," he said. "A woman's supposed

to do housework."

"Says who?"

"Says... I don't know... everyone!" Uncle Pico answered. "It's always been that way."

"So because something's always been a certain way, then that's the right way? Let's go back to child labor then."

"You're just like your parents," he said, sitting back down. "You always have to tell people how smart you are."

Uncle Pico was passed out on the couch by the time Aunt Sazón arrived with Uncle Juke, who was probably just looking for a hot plate of dinner. After them, Ajo, Oregano, and Canelo showed up. They were my cousins. Ajo, the oldest, was twenty. He worked at Tim's Tire Shop near downtown Rey Carlos. The tires he handled had more brains than he did.

There used to be another, older brother. His name was Ismael, but his nickname was Miel, which means honey. He died at seventeen, when I was in second grade. One day, he noticed he was having trouble taking notes at school because his hand wouldn't stop jerking as he wrote. He had a brain tumor. Mom and Dad wired money to Aunt Sazón and Uncle Pico, so they could leave Ecuador and have Miel treated at the Medical Center in Houston. He died six months after they came. I don't remember much about him, but rumor has it Miel was gay and Aunt Sazón and Uncle Pico were ashamed of him. He's buried at Golden Shore Cemetery in downtown Rey Carlos. Even though I don't remember a lot about him, I don't remember anything negative. Miel seemed like he was their best son.

Then there was Oregano who was fifteen. I wasn't looking forward to being in high school with him. Canelo, the youngest, was nine. Compared to his older brothers, he was a genius. But, he was also a whiner.

"Mom, you know I hate GREEEEEN BEEEEANS!" Canelo yelled when Aunt Sazón served him his plate. She immediately took his plate back and served him a fresh one without those horrible green beans he was convinced would ruin his life forever.

"Thanks Mama!" Ajo said. "You make the beeeest food."

"That's right!" Oregano said, chewing on his rice. "The best on the island."

"Hey Ellison," Uncle Juke asked from across the table. "How are your friends?"

"They're okay," I said. "They've been back at school for a while."

"I can't believe Glad Bag got snatched," he said. "She was a nice girl."

"What?" I asked.

"She was doing something," he said, burping. "Modeling! Showing off her goodies. Good girls don't hang around outside. Had she been at home, she would've been safe. Right?"

"Juke, I work," Aunt Sazón piped in.

"Working is fine," Uncle Juke said. "But that's it. A woman can work, but she should go home when work's over."

"Good Lord," I whispered to myself.

"What?" Uncle Juke asked. "You said somethin', Ella?"

"No, just eating."

"Mom! I want more chicken!" Canelo said with a screech that woke up Uncle Pico. Aunt Sazón rushed to the kitchen to grab Canelo more chicken. When she gave it to him, he whined about wanting juice, and off she went to get juice for him. I never understood why she was so... *obedient*. There's nothing wrong with listening to people, but she was being ordered around. Back when I was a little kid, I used to sit in during my parents' lectures at Saint Jerome. Sometimes they taught graduate-level night classes and daycare wasn't open that late, so they'd let me sit in the back of the classroom if I promised to be quiet. Their students were usually nice, paid attention, and did their work. But every once in a while, there would be an asshole and Mom and Dad wouldn't hesitate to send them out the classroom if they acted up. If Mom and Dad could kick adults with no relation to them out of their classes, what was stopping Aunt Sazón from standing up to her family?

"I'm tired, Mom!" Canelo said, his chubby cheeks drooping as he yawned. "Can Dad take me home?"

"C'mon kid," Uncle Pico said, tapping Prince Whine on his back. They took off without saying goodnight. Soon after, Oregano, Ajo, and Juke left, too. Aunt Sazón rubbed her eyes, coughed, and looked at me, as if she was trying to read my mind.

"Uncle Pico said you were *malcriada* with him."

"I was."

"Why? What's wrong with you?"

"He ticked me off," I said.

"Doesn't mean you can be rude."

I was sorry about the tone I used, but I didn't regret anything I said to him. "I'll apologize next time I see him," I said.

Her brown eyes squinted. Her tangled, black hair looked worse than usual. "You'll never get married if you don't change your attitude."

"You mean I'll never find a lazy man who can't bother to make himself a bowl of cereal or kids who treat me like I'm their maid? What a pleasure I'll be missing out on."

She squinted her eyes again and told me to get ready for bed. I never understood why I always got the *be careful or you'll never get married* talk. Nobody ever grabbed Canelo and told him, "Shut up, Canelo. No one wants to marry a whiner like you, so you better quit it." I never heard Aunt Sazón tell Canelo, Oregano, or Ajo they'd get never get married for being idiots. Why was behavior only important for girls? Were girls expected to have dating standards lower than sea level?

As I got ready for bed, I turned on Dad's radio. He got it years ago, way before I was born. It didn't work well, but if I messed with the antenna enough, I could hear channels from Houston and Galveston. My personal favorite was ILAND 103.4. They played old rock music like David Bowie, The Doors, The Rolling Stones, George Harrison, and Janis Joplin. I brushed my teeth to the song "Look Back in Anger" by David Bowie, though the sound quality was awful.

"Elly," Aunt Sazón said, knocking on my door. "Your parents are on the phone."

I shut the radio off and followed Aunt Sazón to the kitchen. It was 2018 and my parents still had a corded phone for emergencies in case our cellphones all died at the same time and we couldn't charge them.

"Elysian!" Dad said. "My girl!"

"How are you, sweetie?" Mom said.

"I'm all right," I said. "Everyone is okay."

"We're glad you survived that horrible shooting," Dad told me. "Our government and their love for guns! When will they think of us?"

"Marcos, we own guns! What are you talking about?" Mom said.

"But when are our politicians going to admit guns kill people?" Dad said. "When, Carmen? When? Guns are horrendous!"

"Mom! Dad! I'm fine. Gladys is missing though."

"What? Glad Bag?" Dad asked.

"*¡Dios Santísimo!*" Mom said. "Do the police know anything?"

"Not much," I said. "She was last seen at Emerald Beach right before the shooting."

"That's horrible!" Mom said. "Be safe, okay? Buenos Aires is beautiful, but Dad and I miss you. We'll be home soon, Elysian. Don't dwell on missing us."

"Do you think the semester might end earlier?" I asked. Mom said it wouldn't. Dad cleared his throat for a minute before he spoke again.

"My girl," he said. "Do you need a lullaby?"

"Marcos, don't do this," Mom said.

"Oh, c'mon. What do you say, Elysian, my heavenly girl?"

"Okay, Dad," I said, laughing a little. "Sing my favorite."

"You got it," he answered. He started singing "Como Te Extraño" by Leo Dan, an Argentine singer he introduced me to when I was little. The song was about missing someone and wanting to see them again, so he'd sing it to me over the phone whenever he was away. Unfortunately, Dad couldn't tell how bad he was at singing.

"Okay, enough," Mom said halfway through the song. "Goodnight, Elysian. I hope you can sleep well after that disaster."

"Night, night, sweet Heaven," Dad said. "We'll try to call you again in a week. Email us anytime, we constantly check our inboxes."

"I will, Dad, goodnight. Goodnight to you, too, Mom."

"Sleep well, sweetie," she said and then hung up.

"It's bedtime," Aunt Sazón told me, her eyes red from exhaustion. "You want me to take you to school tomorrow?"

"Nah, I can walk," I said. "I always do."

"It's supposed to rain tomorrow."

"Eh, I'll catch a ride with Brandon and his dad or something, don't worry about me."

In my room, I tried to fall asleep. I switched positions ten times, counted backwards from 100, and thought about Mr. Garrison's rock lectures. Out of nowhere, I started sweating. My heart sprinted, my body shivered, and my breathing got heavier. Within a minute, Aunt Sazón burst into my room.

"What the heck is going on in here?" she asked. "You were supposed to be asleep two hours ago, Elly."

I tried to answer her, but the only thing I could do was grunt. It was like I forgot how to talk.

"Elly?"

I groaned a second time.

"This is unacceptable, Elly, can't you behave for once?"

"I can't stop this," I said when my voice came back. "I can't stop this. You don't understand, I can't stop this."

Chapter 7

Aunt Sazón was right about the rain. It poured hard as I brushed my teeth. She left me a plate of waffles and turkey bacon for breakfast with a note that said: *If you need me, call me at work, not my cell.* I ate breakfast quickly and called Brandon.

"Yo," he said. "What's happening?"

"Do you think your dad could give me a ride to school today? I was going to walk, but it's raining too much."

"Hold on one sec," he said. "POPS! Elysian needs a ride!"

At 7:15 am, Brandon and Mr. Meyer showed up. Mr. Meyer wore sunglasses though there was no sun yet, but he always did for his glaucoma. He had the typical bouncer look: tattoos, piercings in his ears and a long, black beard. He'd work nights and weekends nonstop. His job was a big part of why his wife divorced him in 2016. She was a receptionist at a dental office. By the time she'd get home, Mr. Meyer would be on his way to work. Brandon said they fought every night because she felt like she had a roommate instead of a husband. After months of fighting, his mother moved to her parents' house in McAllen and mailed divorce papers to Mr. Meyer a week later.

"Doing good, Elysian?" Mr. Meyer asked as I slipped into the backseat of his rusty car.

"Super," I said. "How are you?"

"Tired," he said. "Always am. People never stop clubbing."

"Dad, step on it, we'll be late," Brandon said.

"Like you wanna be on time to school," Mr. Meyer said. As he drove, the rain came down harder and he cursed every curse word I knew.

"It's just rain, Dad," Brandon said.

"I can't see shiiiiiiiiiiiiiiiiiiiit," Mr. Meyer answered. "Bitchin' glaucoma."

"Anything you can do for it?" I asked.

"Bitch about it," he said, which made me laugh.

"Have the surgery, Dad," Brandon said. "If you don't, you'll go blind."

"You got surgery money?" he answered, adjusting his sunglasses. "My deductible is higher than your Uncle Isaiah on Friday nights."

Brandon and I laughed deeply. Mr. Meyer pulled up to the front of the school and we got out fast before we could get caught for skipping the car rider line. We headed to the cafeteria to wait for Tiana and Lalo, but they were already there.

"This rain!" Lalo said. "It's everywhere!"

"Of course it's everywhere," Brandon said. "It's rain, stupid,"

"Don't call me stupid, you butt-muncher!"

"Hey Brandon," Tiana said, batting her eyes. "Good morning."

"Hi there," he answered, unsure of what to say. "Welcome... *to school?*"

When Brandon and I got to geology, Principal Jarmon came on the intercom. He said there was a possible tornado approaching and if it hit, there would be a lockdown. We had tornado drills almost as often as we had fire drills. This wasn't anything new, yet within about thirty seconds, I was sweating. Brandon turned to me and asked if I was okay, but I couldn't answer him.

"Now calm down, Elysian," Mr. Garrison told me. "Don't worry about today's quiz. I'm still going to drop the lowest grade at the end of the semester."

I wasn't a hundred percent sure, but I swore my classmates were staring at me, wondering if I had lost my mind. Brandon put a pencil in my face and asked me what it was. With a light groan, I was able to say, "Pencil."

"You're alert, that's good," he said. "Wanna go to the nurse? I'll walk with you."

Mr. Garrison gave us hall passes and we slowly walked down the hallway and then down the main stairwell. Brandon stayed by my side the whole time. He didn't talk, but he was there and that was enough. When we got to the nurse's office, it was packed with kids who were sneezing and coughing. I sat down in an old chair right outside the office, shaking like hell.

Brandon knelt down in front of me. "How can I help you?"

"What?"

"I want to help you, but I don't know what to do."

"I'm scared," I told him with another light groan.

"What are you scared of?"

"I don't know," I said. The truth was I was scared of everything. I was afraid of people judging my appearance, my personality, my hobbies, my friends, my house, my clothes, and my voice. I was afraid I had a rare disease and I'd die within the next few days. I was afraid of Mom and Dad never coming home even though they always did. I was afraid Gladys was dead and whoever took her would come back and take me, too. I was afraid all the time. *How could I explain my feelings to Brandon? He wouldn't get it.*

"Well," he said. "Are you worried about Gladys?"

I nodded.

"I'm worried about her, too," he said. "The whole city is. I worry about you, too, Elysian. Fear sucks balls, doesn't it?"

"Did you just say fear sucks balls?" I asked, laughing a little.

"I mean, doesn't it?" he said, shrugging his shoulders. "First you're totally okay and then it comes and hits you and you feel scared and you have no idea what to do. I get that way sometimes, too. It sucks balls."

By the time Nurse O'Connor was free, my shakiness had stopped along with my sweating. I could speak easily and my heart didn't feel like it was going to pop out of my chest.

"Sounds like you had a panic attack," Nurse O'Connor said. "Don't worry, they happen. I had a few myself, back in my college days. Are you feeling better now?"

"A lot better, yeah," I answered. She took my blood pressure, pulse, and temperature and since everything was normal, she said I could return to class. Brandon and me walked a little faster since there wasn't much time left in geology and we needed to take the quiz.

"What's a panic attack?" I asked Brandon. "I should've asked Nurse O'Connor, but I forgot."

"Uhm, I'm not sure," he said. "I know they suck, but I don't know why they happen."

Back in class, Mr. Garrison told us to stop by after school to take our quiz. He kept on teaching about rocks, except this time, he kept his eyes on me and he'd smile here and there.

During lunch, Brandon scrolled through his phone. He stumbled on an article that said the Rey Carlos Police Department had a lead on the Emerald Beach Shooting and Gladys Richardson's missing person case.

"News, schmews," Lalo said. "If that was true, my parents and I would've known about it already."

"Maybe your parents already know," Brandon said. "It says someone saw Gladys buy ice cream at Jasper's an hour before the shooting."

"So what?" I said. "Everyone buys ice cream at Jasper's. What else does it say? She was wearing clothes?"

"Man," Brandon said. "RCPD is pretty good for the most part. Remember the serial kidnapper they caught back in 2012?"

"They only got him because he tried kidnapping a kid in front of the police station," Lalo said.

Tiana sat next to us with a tray of mutated green beans, a square slice of pizza, and something pretending to be milk.

"Hey guys," she said, her gaze glued to Brandon. "People are saying the police found out something about Gladys."

"Yeah, they figured out she's missing," Lalo said, rolling his eyes.

"Do you think she ran away?" Tiana said.

"No way," Lalo told her. "She would never run away."

Chapter 8

On Friday night, I stayed home with Uncle Juke because Aunt Sazón had to work a night shift. She was a secretary at Shores Healing, a nursing home close to Southern Texas Hospital. She usually worked a regular day shift, but sometimes she covered for an overnight employee. Uncle Juke cooked a pot of terrible rice and microwaved bland chicken nuggets to go with it. He spent most of the night watching TV, ordering me around the house, and throwing his socks at the wall.

"Boy, this is a boring Friday night!" Uncle Juke said. "Feels like prison!"

"You can say that again," I whispered to myself.

"Huh?"

"Oh, nothing," I said, focusing on the TV. The evening news came on after whatever show Uncle Juke had been watching. The first story of the night was about Gladys. Apparently, someone in Galveston thought he spotted her eating with a man at a restaurant called Gaido's.

"She's a beautiful girl," the man on the news said into the camera. "Pretty. So pretty. You don't forget a girl like her."

After the segment, another reporter came on talking to Mr. Jasper about the Emerald Beach Shooting. The reporter asked him if he planned on moving his ice cream stand to another part of the island for safety.

"Hell no!" Mr. Jasper shouted. "That shooter's gonna have to take me down! I'll wrestle them with my bare hands and pour hot fudge down their eyes! This is Jasper's Ice Cream Stand we're talking about! I ain't no wussy!"

"I'm going to bed," I told Uncle Juke. "Are you sleeping over here tonight?"

"Yeah, on the couch."

"Do you need more covers?"

"I'm good. Night, night. Girls need their beauty sleep."

"Oh yeah," I pretended to agree.

I brushed my teeth, changed into my sleeping clothes, and climbed into bed. Uncle Juke had changed the channel. He must have been watching a naughty show, because I heard him cheering "Excite me, *mujercita*! *¡Quiero ese culo!*" It was clear why he never got married, but no one ever gave him grief for his singlehood.

Since it wasn't that late, I called Lalo. He answered right away and cleared his throat. "Did you watch the news?"

"Yep, I saw. Did you catch Mr. Jasper going wild?"

"Of course," he said. "Are you home alone? I am. My dad just got an emergency call for a bar in downtown."

"No, Uncle Puke is here."

"Aw man, that's worse. Can I come over?"

"Right now? It's dark outside."

"Your uncle can get me, can't he?"

"Well, maybe," I said. "He's in the middle of watching something dirty."

"Oh geez," Lalo said with a hacking sound. "Never mind."

"So," I said, rolling over in my bed. "Do you think Gladys

really went to Galveston?"

"Nope. Galveston is just a bigger Rey Carlos."

"They got Schlitterbahn."

"And we have Tsunami Zone," Lalo said. "I don't know... maybe it was her, but I doubt it. I didn't like the way that dude on the news talked about Gladys. *'You don't forget a girl like her.'* What a creep."

After I got off the phone with Lalo, I tried to sleep, but I couldn't. I looked at the clock on my dresser and saw it was 3:10 in the morning. My phone buzzed with a text from Brandon a second later.

U up?

Yeah.

Thought I heard gunshots.

Where? Are you home?

Nah, Elysian. I'm hanging out with gangbangers.

Brandon!

Did you hear anything?

Only thing I hear outside are crickets doing their thing.

All right, goodnight. Hah. Not me. I'm WIIIIIIDE AWAKE.

Say hi to the gangbangers.

Can't, they already went to prison.

I snuck out of my room slowly. Uncle Juke was passed out with the TV still blaring on the naughty channel. If Mom and Dad knew he had been watching that stuff with me nearby, they'd chase him out of the house with a chainsaw. I went to the kitchen and made a hot cup of tea. As I drank, I looked out the kitchen window. We used to have a curtain over it, until Mom accidentally set it on fire while trying to make cornbread a few months back. There was nothing but darkness and a small amount of shine from the streetlights. I don't know what it was about darkness, but I hated it.

"You like me back, huh?!" Uncle Juke said in his sleep, almost causing me to drop my mug on the floor. "Come over here and I'll show you why they call me Juke."

What a pathetic story that was, I thought to myself. When he was twenty-five and had just moved from Ecuador, the cops busted him at a diner in Corpus Christi after he smashed a jukebox, attempting to steal the change. He didn't do any jail time since he paid the fine.

"You're right," he went on drowsily. "I *am* a stallion."

"Oh my God," I said to myself before retreating back to my bedroom. When I checked my phone, I had more texts from Brandon.

Elysian, I'm watching a doc on this lady who lost her son

Holy crap, she killed him!

Damn! She tried to pin it on the kid's dad!

Instead of texting back, I called him.

"For a good time, call Brandon. How can I help you?"

"What the hell are you doing up so late?"

"Look who's talking," he said. "It's Friday night. I'm watching murder documentaries like always. What are you doing?"

"Trying to sleep. Uncle Puke is talking to women in his dreams."

"He might as well—it's not like he can talk to them at any other time. I'm home by myself. Dad gets home soon though."

"Don't you get scared of being alone at night? It'd creep me out," I said.

"Nope, I've seen so many murder docs, I know how to protect myself. My wallet saved my ass. Literally."

"Night, Brandon."

"Sleep well, Elysian."

It was 4:30 in the morning when I fell asleep. I woke up to Uncle Juke making breakfast. He banged on pots, cursed out loud, then burned himself with oil and screamed bloody murder.

"You awake yet, Ella?!" Uncle Juke called out. "Breakfast is... *kinda* ready!"

I brushed my teeth, straightened my hair, and went to the kitchen. Uncle Juke had made sloppy pancakes, burned sausages, and a greenish smoothie which smelled awful.

"Uh," I said. "Thanks."

"Oh, this is crap, isn't it?" he asked. "C'mon, let's go to Prince Griddle's."

I changed into black shorts and a red t-shirt and got into the backseat of Uncle Juke's car, which was older than Pangea. There were empty cigarette boxes all over the floor mixed with empty bottles of soda. His ancient air freshener, a half-naked woman blowing a kiss, bounced as he drove. He had had that air freshener ever since I was in first grade. Every time Dad saw it, he'd tell him to throw it out, but Uncle Juke never listened to anyone.

"Did you sleep well?" Uncle Juke asked while we sat at a red light.

"Decently."

"I slept excellent," he answered. "Had some good dreams, too. Did you have any dreams? I dream every night."

"No," I said. "I don't dream a lot, never have."

"Not even about... boys?"

"Nope."

"Why in the hell not? You do like boys, right?"

"Sure," I said. I had liked boys forever, at least since third grade, maybe before then. But if I had a car, I wouldn't have an air freshener of a man in a speedo blowing a kiss.

"There's gotta be a boy you like," Uncle Juke said, passing through the green light. "You're almost in high school."

"I've had crushes," I said, fiddling with my seatbelt.

"When I was your age, I had already lost my virginity," he said. I wasn't sure if he wanted me to clap or grab pom-poms and cheer for him. "Oh, it was fantastic... the best ever! She was twenty, I think. What a slut, huh? Doing it with a fourteen year old boy like me."

"Are you serious?" I said, wanting to shove his air freshener down his throat. "She's a slut? Did she know you were fourteen?"

"I looked old for my age. I lied and told her I was eighteen."

"So, you lied to her, she thought you were an adult, and she's the slut? You're so full of it, Uncle Juke. This is why women don't date you for very long. No woman likes an asshole."

"No man likes a woman who's disrespectful, Elly," he said.

"I'm disrespectful? Look at your air freshener." He opened his mouth like he was about to speak up, but didn't.

When we got to Prince Griddle's, it was packed. The wait was forty-five minutes and by the time we got a table, it was almost lunchtime. I ordered two egg and potato breakfast tacos with a glass of orange juice. Uncle Juke got the special which was a big plate of pancakes, biscuits, sausage, bacon, grits, and a tall cup of creamed coffee. As he ate, grease flowed from the corners of his mouth to his shirt, but he never bothered to wipe himself.

"What?" he asked when he caught me staring. "Never seen a man eat?"

"Not like *that*," I answered.

"Boy, you got some nerve. I wonder why your parents raised you so badly."

"They're barely home, it's not their fault," I said. It was supposed to be a joke, but then I realized it was true. They were almost never home. If they weren't teaching at Saint Jerome's, they were teaching at another university or traveling to give a guest lecture. When they were home, it was for a few hours to wind down before going to bed and doing their jobs again in the morning. I started to wonder who really raised me.

When I was much younger, Abuela Rosemary lived with us in the house. Dad was her only child and she had him later in life, so when I was little, she was already in her eighties. Not long after moving in with us, she died from old age. She never, ever called me weird, strange, or *malcriada*. Her English wasn't the best. Her Ecuadorian accent was thick and hard. But she always said "Elysian" perfectly. Maybe I'd be different if she were still alive. Maybe I wouldn't be weird. Maybe I'd be happier. Maybe I wouldn't have those panic attacks Nurse O'Connor mentioned.

"Are you done?" Uncle Juke asked with more grease oozing down his face.

"Yeah," I said, even though I had barely touched my tacos.

"You sure? Your aunt's gonna bitch at me if you didn't eat enough."

"I'm fine," I assured him. "Can you drop me off at Lalo's?"

Uncle Juke wiped his face with a paper napkin, paid the check, and walked me outside to his car. I texted Lalo to let him know I was coming over.

Good, I'm alone he texted back.

Still?

My mom had to help my grandpa with his new computer and my dad is on another call.

Oh, okay, I'll be there soon.

"Lalo's house," Uncle Juke announced when we arrived.

"Make sure you call your aunt and tell her where you are, okay? I'm heading home."

He sped off the second Lalo opened the door. It was past noon and Lalo was still in his pajamas, hair uncombed, stubble around his chin and upper lip. His eyes drooped at the corners.

"I'm so tired," he said.

"Me too," I told him. "I think I slept four hours, but maybe less. Anything new about Gladys?"

"Same tip we heard on the news last night."

"Have you or your parents talked to Octavio?" I asked, taking a seat at the little kitchen table, which was sticky with jelly residue. "Wouldn't he know something?"

"Octavio's brain is smaller than an ant's foot. I think my parents have talked to him, but I haven't. He's a jerk."

"Doesn't he work at Retro World?"

"I haven't heard anything about him quitting."

"Then let's go," I said.

"Now? I'm in pajamas."

"Well change your clothes, doofus."

"Fine, fine," Lalo said, scratching his head. "Hold on right here." He walked off to his bedroom.

His house was way smaller than mine and much older, too. My house was in the newer part of the neighborhood, close to the splash pad for little kids. Lalo's part was the original Wendell Green Estates, built back in the 1970s during the Vietnam War. The wallpaper was so tacky, it would give any interior designer an instant heart attack. The air vents were blocked with thick dust, which was ironic since Mr. Richardson was obsessed with air conditioning. You'd think he'd take care of his own air vents. The kitchen was the coolest part of the house. The black and white checkered floor went well with the vintage feel. The bright red refrigerator was round at the edges, a perfect match for the bright red toaster on the counter. Lalo once told me the fridge and toaster came with the house and they still worked decently.

"I'm ready," Lalo said, wearing jeans, a gray Houston Astros shirt, and a blue baseball cap.

We walked out the door and made a right onto Travis Avenue. Retro World was half a mile away. It was a 50s style diner, bakery, and gift shop under one roof. They had everything broke kids like us would enjoy: free movie nights, raffles, cheap food specials, and ice cream socials. But we never went because Lalo didn't want to run into Octavio.

"Man, it's burning hot today," Lalo said, sweating already.

"We live in Texas."

"Sadly," he said. "My cousin Eliza who lives in New York said it's like 70 degrees up there right now."

"Whatever," I said. "We're stuck here until we can get out."

"Wherever you move, I'm going with you."

"What if I moved to some place far away like the islands of Java?"

"I'd go," he said. "I'd go anywhere with you."

Retro World was dead when we got there. Besides us, there were three people at a small table sharing a massive brownie.

"What will y'all have?" a waitress with red eyes asked us.

"Uh, we're actually looking for Octavio. Is he here today?"

"Cooking in the back," she said. "Wait a sec and I'll get him for ya."

Lalo and I skimmed through the menu even though we only had a few dollars. Octavio approached us after a few minutes, smelling of spices and cologne stronger than Muhammad Ali. His black hair was gelled tightly, his cheeks red like Lalo's fridge, and his brown eyes were half-open.

"What's up?" he asked. He punched Lalo on the arm in a playful way. Lalo squirmed in his seat and rubbed his arm gently.

"We wanted to know if you knew anything else about Gladys," I said.

"I haven't slept well since she's been gone," he said with his eyes looking down at his ragged shoes. "The last thing she said to me was 'I love you.'"

"That's what she told me, too," Lalo said. "I miss my sister."

"If you hear anything from her, let me know," Octavio said. "I just hope she's alive."

"I'm sure she is," I said. My emotions had been unpredictable, but something told me Gladys was alive. I wasn't sure if she was okay, but my gut told me she was alive. I didn't know where she was and I wished I did. *Where could she have gone? Why would someone take her? Why would anyone want to hurt her?*

"I gotta get back to work," Octavio said, sneezing into his arm. "If I hear anything, I'll call." He hastily adjusted his hairnet and walked away quickly.

"Let's get out of here before they make us order something," Lalo said. We left, unsure of where to go next. The heat seemed stronger than earlier.

"Wanna come over?" I asked Lalo. "I think my aunt's working again this morning. We can hang out until she shows up."

"What if she finds out? Won't she flip if you're alone with a boy?"

"She won't find out," I said. "Just don't make it obvious you came over."

We went to my house, sweating buckets by the time we walked inside. Lalo sat down on the couch and panted heavily.

"Are you okay?" I asked him.

"I'm thirsty," he said. "Water."

"Coming up."

I dashed to the kitchen, opened the fridge, grabbed a bottle of water, and rushed back to him. He twisted the cap off and chugged the water down so fast, I thought he'd choke.

"It's too hot," he said. "Do you have ice cream?"

"Uncle Juke ate all of it last night."

"Dang. I'd say let's go get some, but I don't wanna go back out."

"We can freeze grapes," I said. "My parents do that when it's real hot."

While we waited for the grapes to freeze, we got on the desktop computer in the living room. We checked all of Gladys' social media accounts, but there wasn't anything new. Her friends had posted comments saying "we miss you" and "where are you?" Her fans on Instagram said they wanted to start a search party across the United States. I didn't realize how much I missed Gladys until I read those comments. After she moved out of Lalo's house to live with Octavio, I had barely seen her. She wasn't my big sister, but I still missed her a lot.

"I hate this," Lalo said as he read the comments. "Why is she gone? Brandon's told me enough murder mystery facts for me to know she's never coming home again."

"Brandon reads and watches too much of that stuff," I said. "He's probably gonna end up being a detective someday."

"He can start now then. Since he loves mysteries so much, maybe he can look for Gladys."

"You're right. He can."

"Really?" Lalo said. "How would Brandon do that?"

"Let's call him."

I texted Brandon first before calling him. He texted me back instantly and said *Yeah, you can call, let me pause my movie.* I asked him to come over to my house if he wasn't too entertained by his movie.

"Nah, it's just *Pulp Fiction*," he said. "Seen it a thousand times."

"What? Your dad lets you watch Quentin Tarantino movies?" I asked.

"He's asleep during the day. I got freedom to do whatever until he wakes up."

Brandon arrived within half an hour. He brought his tablet and connected to the Wi-Fi.

"Nothing new on her pages," Brandon said after checking Gladys' social media accounts. "You know what she was wearing, Lalo?"

"A sundress. Sandals. Regular beach clothes. It's in her selfie, dummy."

"Why was she alone?" Brandon asked. "Why didn't she go to the beach with Octavio?"

"I dunno, maybe he had to work," Lalo said.

"Aha!" Brandon said. "Okay, she posted a picture of herself while she waited for the photographer. She was distracted."

"So?" Lalo said.

"Can't be distracted out in public," Brandon said. "That's how you get killed."

"C'mon Brandon, lots of people get distracted," I said.

"But if you get distracted too much, you're an easy target. Bobby Dunbar was four years old and the guy who was supposed to be watching him got distracted and he was never found."

"Quit it, Brandon, you're scaring me," Lalo said, squirming his upper body.

"It's true," Brandon said, saving his notes on the tablet. "But, I'm gonna be honest with you. I think she's all right. Gladys is smart. It's easier to kidnap a dumbass."

"Brandon!" I said. "Good God."

"I saw one case on TV where this kid in Chicago was snatched during his walk home from school. He sang the same song over and over again until the kidnappers kicked him out of the car. If that kid was dumb, he'd be dead."

"Okay, enough mystery talk," I said. "My aunt will be home soon. She'll freak if she knows I was home alone with two boys."

"If I see her, I'll tell her we were sacrificing chickens to the gods," Brandon said.

"Shut up and get out of here. You too, Lalo."

"Me? I'm the good one," Lalo said. "Let's go, Brandon."

"Bye guys," I said as they headed out. I locked the door behind them and flipped the TV on to the news. The reporters were talking about a walk for charity that had raised over $100,000. The next story was about an old woman who knocked a burglar into a coma with her cane when he broke into her house.

"He came in my house and I said, *Lord Jesus, give me the strength. I'm the queen of my castle. Ain't no thieving son of a bitch gonna dethrone me!*"

I laughed, but felt my heart pacing. Soon enough, my breathing was as fast as my heart. Then I got stiff. I started crying, sweating, and screaming at the same time. Aunt Sazón walked in, dropped her purse on the floor, and ran to me.

"Ella, what happened?"

"I can't feel my hands," I said through the horrible sensations. "I can't feel my feet."

"Breathe," she said. "Breathe easy. Make believe you're at the beach."

"Not the beach!" I said. "Not the beach. Not the beach!"

"What's wrong with the beach?" she asked.

"Not the beach!" I cried out. "I hate the beach!"

"Okay, then a pool," she said over me. "A nice, warm pool. It has a slide just for you. You go down and land in the center of the water. It covers you in warm waves. It's the best pool you've ever been in. The temperature is perfect, the water is clear, the waves are gentle, and they rock you like you're a baby."

For a moment, I wished I could be a baby again. All I'd think about is eating and sleeping. When Mom and Dad found out they were going to be parents, they wanted me to have a heavenly name. They searched through dictionaries, thesauruses, and baby name books. And out of everything they found in those books, they picked Elysian from Elysian Fields, a beautiful paradise in Greek mythology where heroes went after they died. I had a heavenly name for no reason. My mind was always in hell.

Chapter 9

After my last episode, Aunt Sazón took a leave of absence from work to stay home with me. She'd be there when I woke up, when I got home from school, and when I went to bed. The upside was not having to see Uncle Juke or Uncle Pico as often.

Aunt Sazón was nice at first. She'd get up early to make a gourmet breakfast, typically consisting of eggs, bacon, and buttered garlic toast. Sometimes she threw in chocolate chip pancakes and a glass of freshly squeezed orange juice. One Thursday morning, she sat by me at the table while I chowed down on another gourmet breakfast.

"How long have you been having these episodes?" she asked.

"I don't know. A while," I answered. "They came out of nowhere."

"I used to worry a lot when I was your age. You know what I did? I'd play with my dolls or put on makeup."

"Not a fan."

"Well, what do you like to do?"

"Hang out with my friends," I told her. "Listen to old rock music. Read. Write." Aunt Sazón had known me my entire life and had butted in for most of it—how could she not know what I liked to do for fun?

"A girl your age shouldn't be cooped up at home," she said. "No wonder you're having these episodes. You need to get out more. You need girlfriends, too. It won't do you any good to hang out with boys like Lalo and Brandon, they can't talk to you about girl topics."

"What are girl topics?"

"Cute boys, makeup, purses, nails, you know, the things women like. Maybe if you try those things out, you'll like them."

The answer was still no.

After breakfast, I walked to school. When I got there, Tiana snuck up from behind and hugged me. She wore dark lipstick, a black skirt, and a plaid blouse.

"Elysian! I haven't seen you in a while."

"I've been around."

"We need to hang out," she said. "How about this weekend? We can go to Retro World."

"Uhm," I said, wanting to say no way in hell. Then, I thought back to the time Tiana made me tea and how she listened to me without giving her unwanted opinion.

"Yeah," I said. "Do you want to invite Lalo and Brandon?"

"Nah, let's make it a girls' day. It'll be fun! I can't wait. Let me put it on my Google calendar, so I don't forget."

"Uhhh, yeah... calendars are always helpful."

"You're hilarious," she said. "I'll see you later, okay? I have to run to Book Club."

"See you later."

Within five minutes, Lalo and Brandon arrived. They both grabbed cinnamon rolls and milk for breakfast and gobbled everything up.

"I'm so hungry, I'm gonna eat the whole school," Lalo said. "My parents still haven't gone grocery shopping. All we have in the fridge is jelly."

"At least you got jelly," Brandon said. "You know what we got? Wheat bread."

"What's wrong with wheat bread?" I asked.

"C'mon, Elysian. The devil made wheat bread."

"No," I said. "Wheat bread made the devil."

The first bell rang and we hurried to class. Brandon walked close to me. He kept his hands tight on his backpack straps as we shoved our way up the main stairwell. I noticed a big zit on his forehead that looked like it was going to pop any second.

"Are you staring at my zit?" he asked when we got to geology.

"I mean, it's big. I can't help it."

"Elysian, it's just a zit. Calm down."

"It's gonna pus out any second!"

"Yeah, man! All over your desk too, girl."

During Mr. Garrison's lecture, I thought about Mom and Dad. I thought about Gladys and whether or not she was hurt. I even thought about Abuela Rosemary and I almost never thought about her. Then, I thought about my uncles, my cousins, and Aunt Sazón. They were there for me every time Mom and Dad traveled, but did they enjoy it? I assumed they couldn't have since they always commented on how different I was. It was obvious they were uncomfortable around me.

"Hey Elysian," Brandon said, tapping me on the back. "Class is over."

"Huh?"

"The bell rang."

"When?"

"A second ago," he said. "Let's go."

Brandon and I walked out and he rushed in the opposite direction to English class. I sat in my assigned seat behind Lalo in math class, who was sweating and coughing.

"We got a quiz today, don't we?"

"Yeah," I answered. "Don't be surprised, it's on the class calendar."

"I didn't study."

"Well, hopefully it won't be too hard."

"You serious? Bautista is harder than rocks!"

"What?" a confused Ms. Bautista said from her desk. "I'm as hard as a rock?"

"Not you," Lalo said, clearing his throat. "The math."

Unfortunately, the math was super hard. I didn't even know how to start solving half of the questions, and for the other half, I just guessed. Lalo didn't even bother. He wrote his name and turned in the quiz totally blank, so he could earn the standard fifteen points.

"Who uses math?" he asked when time was up.

"A lot of people."

"Losers."

"Astronauts, architects, engineers," I said. "They're not losers."

"Nerds, then."

"Nerds who make the big bucks."

"Hell, I can make big bucks by dealing crack."

"Lalo!" I laughed so hard, Ms. Bautista warned me with detention if I didn't quiet down. She taught us how to find the slope of a line. I took a lot of notes, but didn't understand anything I was writing.

Lunch was different. Tiana brought her friend Nate to eat with us. Nate's full name was Nathan Lane, like the actor. He moved to Rey Carlos Island in sixth grade. I didn't know a lot about him except he was originally from Galveston.

"Nate loves murder mysteries too, Brandon," Tiana said, licking her lips. "Right, Nate?"

"Oh yeah," he said shakily. "Love 'em. Favorite killer is the Zodiac."

"Zodiac?" Brandon said. "That's nothing. I bet you a million dollars the Zodiac was multiple people. Best killer out there was whoever got the German family at Hinterkaifeck Farm. Killer hid in the attic, man... and then one night, *chop*!"

"Whoa okay," Lalo said, eating some of his chips. "Enough murder talk, please."

"You don't think that's cool, dude?" Brandon asked as Nate gulped deeply. Even Tiana started sweating from her forehead.

"I mean, I guess," Lalo said. "But that poor family. Can you imagine just minding your own business and then someone hacks up you like you're a piece of food?"

"Some way to go," Brandon answered. "Cause of death: hacked by an unknown hacker."

"Neat," Nate said, still shaky.

"You have a lot of knowledge on that subject," Tiana said, licking her lips. "Do you think you'll be an investigator or something one day?"

"Me? Maybe," Brandon said. "I could investigate why it's like eleven bucks to go to the damn movies."

It was cloudy when school let out, but I made it home before the rain poured. Aunt Sazón was in the kitchen, wiping the granite counters.

"Hey there," she said. "How was school?"

"Fine."

"What did you learn?"

"Math is hard," I said, turning my back to her.

"Elly," she said, clearing her throat. "We need to talk."

"About?"

"Sit," she said, pulling out a chair from the kitchen table for me. She poured a glass of apple juice for herself, and then sat to enlighten me with her wisdom.

"I talked to Uncle Pico earlier," she said. "He has important concerns."

"Oh boy, we better call the Supreme Court."

"Elly," she said, firmly. "I want you to know your family loves you."

"What is this about?"

"Are you..." she said, squirming in her seat and clearing her throat. "Are you gay?"

"No."

"Really?" she said, her lips tight and eyebrows raised. "You're not?"

"Would it matter if I was?"

"I don't think it would."

"Yeah it would," I said. "Every little thing I don't do your way is such a huge deal. Guess what, Aunt Sazón? Not everyone is meant to be like you or your family. People are different. Just because you think girls have to do things a certain way, doesn't mean it's written in God's blood somewhere. You're not the leader of the world."

"I'm trying to help you," she said, sitting back in her chair. "There's something off about you and you need to fix it. I'm not sure what it is, but it needs repair now so you can grow out of it. I'm on *your* side."

"That is such bull, Aunt Sazón!" I said, standing up. "Instead of focusing on me, why don't you teach your sons how to be useful?"

"This is exactly why your parents always leave!" she said,

pointing in my face. "If I had a daughter like you, I'd travel whenever I could! I'm only trying to help!"

"Help me with what?" I asked.

"Everything! If you acted like a normal girl for five days, I guarantee you'd be happier. Those panic attacks you have will go away. That's why you're having them, Elly. When people act the way you do, their brains get messed up. Trust me. You keep this attitude up and someday, you might turn into a lesbian."

"Turn into a lesbian?" I said, laughing as I patted my hand on my chest. "Gay people aren't Transformers. You'll never see Optimus Prime at the Pride Parade."

"You're a smart mouth, too," she said. "No one likes a smart mouth."

"Nobody likes a dumb mouth either."

Aunt Sazón sent me to my room and I heard her talking to my parents. Every time she talked on the phone, she talked loud enough for people in Samoa to hear her. She said I was out of control, defiant, grumpy, and not acting like myself. There was truth in that though. Something was wrong with me. The panic attacks showed up whenever they wanted to. But I didn't think they had anything to do with my personality. How come Aunt Sazón was allowed to be overbearing? How come Uncle Pico was allowed to be a dick? How come Uncle Juke could be disgusting about women? Weren't those problem behaviors? Why was I the only one in the family who needed to change?

"Ella!" Aunt Sazón said, pounding her fist on my door. "Your parents are on the phone."

I opened my door, saw her heated expression, and rushed to the kitchen to talk on the unnecessary landline.

"Elysian!" Dad said. "What's the deal? Why are you being difficult? Something up?"

"How come I can't be myself?" I asked.

"No one said you couldn't," Mom said. "But you need to respect people, especially your aunt. She's done so much for you."

"Yeah, she's done *a lot*," I said sarcastically.

"Two and a half more months, Elysian," Dad said. "She's a nag, I get it. But try not to kill your aunt."

"I'll try."

"Please behave, Elysian," Mom said. "Aunt Sazón has different ideas than you, but that's okay. It's what makes the world interesting."

"Sure."

They blew me goodnight kisses and we hung up. When I turned around, Aunt Sazón stood behind me, shaking her head. "What do you want for dinner?"

"I thought I was grounded."

"You are, but you still need to eat. This isn't Alcatraz."

"Spaghetti?"

"Good choice. Your uncles and cousins are coming over."

"Joy to the world."

While Aunt Sazón cooked, I worked on homework in my room. I finished around six, plopped myself into my bed, and got a text from Lalo.

What's up, I've been messaging you on Twitter.

I'm grounded.

No way! What's your punishment? Listening to her talk?

You're funny. But no, I'm not allowed to go out this weekend.

Boooooooooooo.

She didn't take my phone away though. She said a phone is an emergency tool.

More like she's a tool.

I laughed and put my pillow over my mouth to quiet myself. The doorbell rang three times, the way Uncle Pico always rang it.

"Ella!" Aunt Sazón called out from the kitchen. "Open the door!"

When I opened the door, Uncle Pico, Ajo, Oregano, and Canelo barged inside without saying hello. Uncle Juke came two or three minutes later. I was hungry before they came, but once they arrived, I lost my appetite. Aunt Sazón served Uncle Pico first, then Ajo, Oregano, Canelo, and Uncle Juke. She served me and herself last.

"Niece," Uncle Pico said to me. "Heard you had a rough day today."

"Not really."

"How's school?" Uncle Juke asked. "What do they teach kids these days?"

"Same stuff. Math, science, English, electives," I said, twirling some spaghetti with my fork.

"Do they have Home Ec at your school?" Aunt Sazón asked. "You could learn how to cook and sew and make pies."

"There's a worthy class," Uncle Juke said. "You need to learn that stuff, so you'll know it when you get married."

"Right," I said, sighing. "Can't wait."

"Marriage is great," Uncle Pico said. "Isn't it, Katarina?"

"It's wonderful," she said, wiping her face with a napkin.

"When I met Katarina, she was nineteen. Full of life, happiness, and attention. I knew she'd make a good wife."

"Oh yeah," I said. "That's what every woman wants to be: a wife."

"Now you're getting the idea," Uncle Pico said, nodding. "Think about your actions now or you might not get a husband later."

"I WANT ICE CREAM!" Canelo said with a screech. "NOW!"

Aunt Sazón immediately got up to get him a bowl of ice cream.

"I haven't heard anything about Glad Bag lately," Ajo piped in.

"Me either," Oregano said. "Too bad. She was hooooooooot."

"Yeah! The things I'd do to her!" Ajo said.

"That girl isn't proper," Uncle Pico said, chewing on his last bit of spaghetti. "What was she thinking getting into modeling? She's a married woman. Married women don't need to show off their bodies."

"Finally, someone said it," Uncle Juke agreed. "I bet she was cheating on Octavio with that photographer. She always seemed loose to me."

"Whoa, how interesting," I said, standing up from the table. "I am suddenly very sleepy and need to go to bed. Goodnight, everyone."

"Are you sure? Your bedtime isn't for a while," Aunt Sazón said with Canelo, complaining about how he didn't have sprinkles in his ice cream.

"I'm exhausted," I said. "Goodnight."

After I got ready for bed, I stayed up, scrolling through my phone. I Googled articles about Gladys, but didn't find anything new except for blog posts written by her fans. Some were convinced her abduction was a scheme to promote her modeling career.

In the middle of the night, I lied in bed wide awake. I had to be up for school in a couple of hours. Aunt Sazón slept in Mom and Dad's bedroom whenever they traveled, far away from my room even though she snored loud enough for people in New Zealand to hear her. I got out of bed and headed to the kitchen to make myself a hot cup of tea. When it cooled enough, I slowly sipped the bittersweet liquid.

The house was quiet. It felt like I was home alone, like an orphan or a single lady with her own empty house. I had never been bothered with the possibility of not getting married, but I was terrified at the prospect of being alone. I didn't always need someone with me, but it was nice to have a person around when I needed company. Lalo and Brandon were the best company. Mom and Dad were good company, but they weren't around much and when they were, they were busy. I didn't hate them for their careers. I thought it was nice they chose their paths when everyone said they couldn't make their dreams happen.

Dad was an only child. He was born in Otavalo, Ecuador, a smallish city back in the day. Abuela Rosemary had a one-night stand with her neighborhood's bakery owner, Mr. César Muñoz and gave birth to Dad nine months later. César didn't want anything to do with them, so Abuela Rosemary immediately changed Dad's name from Marcos César Muñoz to Marcos Ramón Lecaro, using her father's middle and last names.

Mom was in a similar spot. She grew up in Guayaquil, a big city in Ecuador, the same city where I was born. When she was a kid, she loved playing school with her stuffed animals. She'd sit them in rows and use a piece of cardboard as the blackboard. She grew up poor like Dad. When she finished high school, she wanted to go to college. That choice banned her from the family for years. She was seen as a traitor who didn't want to help her family, especially by Uncle Juke and Aunt Sazón. When Mom enrolled at a university and got a job with the registration office, she saw an ad for a room for rent close to her school. The landlord was Abuela Rosemary. Dad was living there, too. Mom married her landlord's son. It was the corniest romance ever.

I didn't hate my parents for their careers. They had worked hard for them. But sometimes I wished they didn't have any kids. If they didn't have time for a life outside of teaching, why have a family in the first place?

When I finished my tea, I snuck to my room and tried to sleep. I counted the books on my bookcase forward and backward. I closed my eyes and thought about one of Mr. Garrison's lectures. I recited the quadratic formula multiple times. Nothing worked. By the time I finally felt sleepy, Aunt Sazón banged on my door. "Elly! Get up and go! It's Friday!"

"*Dios Santo*," I said to myself. "Okay, I'm getting up!"

While I brushed my teeth and combed my hair, Aunt Sazón blasted Elvis Crespo, her favorite singer. He was known for his extremely repetitive song called "Suavemente," but it always gave me the creeps. It was basically about a dude who wants to make out nonstop.

"Good morning!" she said through the chorus. "We're having pancakes!"

"Great," I answered, but she didn't hear me. I sat down at the kitchen table, already set with syrup, butter, and powdered sugar. When the song ended, Aunt Sazón shut the radio off and served me my plate.

"Are you excited? The weekend is here," she said.

"I'm grounded."

"Oh yeah, that's right."

"Can I ask you something?"

"You can ask me anything," she said, which wasn't entirely true.

"Do you ever wish my mom were different?"

"What do you mean?"

"Like, do you ever wish she hadn't gone to college and gotten a job to help the family?"

"That was years ago, Ella," Aunt Sazón said, swallowing a piece of pancake. "If that's what she wanted to do, that's fine."

"Was it?" I said, looking at her. Of course it wasn't fine. If it was, Mom wouldn't have been kicked out of the house.

"We were worried about her," Aunt Sazón said. "I was, Uncle Juke was, your grandparents were hurt. We thought she'd go to college and never find a good job. It happens a lot in Ecuador. Many young people graduate from college, but there aren't enough jobs for everyone. We thought her life was over."

"So why kick her out of the house? Wouldn't that have made life worse on her?"

"Well, if we hadn't kicked her out, she would've never met your dad. Aren't you hungry?" Aunt Sazón asked ten minutes into breakfast after I had only eaten a tiny bit of my food.

"Not really," I said. "I can take this for lunch."

"Go ahead, there are clean containers in the dishwasher."

I got up, grabbed one, and shoved the pancakes into the container. I put on my backpack and snatched my keys from the hook by the front door.

"I'm out," I said. "See ya later."

"Remember to come straight home. You're grounded until Monday."

"I know."

At the school courtyard, the first person I ran into was Nate. He was so focused on reading a book, he didn't hear me saying hello to him. By the time he looked up, I was already walking away.

"Hey, wait," he said, running to me. "I'm sorry, this book is good."

"What are you reading?"

"Uhm, it's called *Al Capone Does My Shirts*. So, Tiana was telling me the other day that your dad's a biology professor?"

"Yes, he teaches genetics, but he majored in biology."

"Can he help me with homework?"

"He's in Buenos Aires with my mom. She teaches anthropology."

"Dang, I'm screwed. If your dad knows biology, you might know something right?"

"Nope," I answered. "I'm in geology. I thought it'd be easier."

"Ugh, I'm gonna find Tiana. Maybe she can help. Do you think we can study together sometime?"

"Why? We're in different science classes."

"We're in some of the same classes," he said, shrugging and shaking at the same time. "Well, I gotta go. I'll see you later."

He took off in the opposite direction. I went inside the cafeteria and found Brandon and Lalo by the vending machines. Lalo was wearing a new t-shirt with a picture of Gladys. Her smile was contagious, but my mind said her smile was gone forever.

"Are you okay?" Lalo said. I didn't realize I was having another attack until I fell flat on the cold floor. Brandon and Lalo picked me up and carried me to Nurse O'Connor's office. The morning bell rang, but they didn't leave my side. I lied on the recovery couch with my breath and heart pulsing so fast, my face and chest burned.

"Elysian?" Nurse O'Connor said, patting my forehead with a wet washcloth. "Breathe. In and out. Like this, iiiiiiiiiiin, ooooooooooout."

"I can't do it," I said. "I'm scared."

"What are you scared of?" Brandon asked. "You can tell us."

"Tell us everything," Lalo said. "Anything you want."

"I'm scared," I said. "I'm dying."

"What?!" Lalo said with a gasp. "What do you mean you're dying? What happened?"

"You sick or something?" Brandon asked.

"No," I said, feeling my face swell. "I don't know. My body feels like it's dying."

"You're not dying, Elysian," Nurse O'Connor said. "This is a panic attack. It's okay, a lot of people have them. Your body is working for you, not the other way around."

"What are you talking about?" I asked through my tears.

"You're breathing hard because your body is giving you more oxygen," she said. "Your body's in fight or flight mode."

Lalo and Brandon sat down by me during the entire attack. They tried telling me jokes, but that didn't work, so Brandon told me a story instead. "Once upon a time," he said. "There was a broom in a house. It had never been used, so one day, it got fed up and came to life. Then it bashed in its owner's skull for being a damn dirty dumb ass!"

"Good Lord, Brandon!" Lalo said.

But after that horrible story, my breathing slowed down. The feeling in my hands and feet returned, too. Nurse O'Connor took my blood pressure and pulse to make sure I was okay enough to go to class. She smiled as she showed me my numbers.

"See?" she said. "You're okay. Panic attacks make you feel like you're not, but you are."

"Are you sure?" I asked.

"Very sure," she said. "You are fine. I know it's hard, but try to remember that for the rest of today."

Lalo, Brandon, and I walked to class. We were stopped by Principal Jarmon, but we showed him our hall passes from Nurse O'Connor.

"All of you were sick?" he asked.

"Yeah, Principal J," Brandon told him. "We were puking everywhere. Oh, man. I think I feel it coming back right now."

"Get to class," Principal Jarmon said. "This is a place of learning, not vomiting."

In math, Ms. Bautista expanded on her last lesson. We were learning the order of operations, also known as PEMDAS. To remember the acronym, Ms. Bautista taught us "Please excuse my dear Aunt Sally." Lalo's version was "Please excuse my dang ass shakin'," which made me laugh out loud during class way too many times.

"Richardson, Lecaro," Ms. Bautista said, rolling her eyes. "Enough."

After school, I went home like Aunt Sazón asked. I found her in the kitchen, stirring a spoon in a big pot. She wore a shiny, purple dress and matching shoes.

"What's the occasion?" I asked.

"It's my wedding anniversary," she said. "Uncle Pico is coming over for dinner."

"Oh, nice. I need a nap."

"Go ahead," she told me. "Rest."

I went into my bedroom, threw myself on my bed, and fell asleep. When I woke up at seven in the evening, I was dripping with sweat. I tried to breathe, but suddenly burst into tears. Out of nowhere, I thought about Miel and how he had died unexpectedly. *Maybe my brain is malfunctioning, too. Did I have a tumor? Am I going to die like he did? What if my brain is dying? Are there any good brain surgeons on Rey Carlos Island?* I grabbed my phone and Googled brain tumor symptoms, but I couldn't read the results because I cried the thickest tears ever. I shook in my bed as my thoughts raced. I clenched my blankets and accepted I had a massive brain tumor and there was no cure and

I was going to die within the next week. All I wanted was silence in my mind, even if it was only for a single minute. More tears drizzled down my face as I hyperventilated. I was so scared, but there was nothing I could do.

Chapter 10

On Saturday morning, I woke up at three o'clock. My house was quiet except for the TV in the living room where Aunt Sazón and Uncle Pico had fallen asleep on the couch. They looked adorable for once, probably because they weren't talking.

I tiptoed to the kitchen for a snack since I had slept through dinner. My stomach grumbled, but thankfully Aunt Sazón and Uncle Pico didn't hear anything. I grabbed a cereal bar and a juice pouch before tiptoeing back to my bedroom. Once inside, I gobbled my snack as quietly as possible. I was about to get back in bed, when my phone buzzed.

Hey! Are you awake? Lalo asked.

Yep.

Me too.

I can tell.

Shut up, Elysian!

I'm gonna push you!

The rest of his texts were about Gladys. Someone in Corpus Christi thought they saw her eating lunch at U&I Restaurant. Then again, Gladys had several sighting reports. She had some in Houston, some in Galveston, some in Austin, a few in San Antonio, and most recently, one up in Denver, Colorado. I started to wonder if she really went missing after all. *Did she take off because she needed a change of scenery? Was she tired of Octavio? Was she fed up with being called Glad Bag every time she visited her old neighborhood?* Her love for Lalo was the clearest thing about her. There was no way in hell she'd leave without letting him know where she was. For the most part, I liked being an only child, but if someone were to put a gun to my head and tell me I needed to pick someone in the world to be my sibling, I would pick Gladys without a second thought.

Okay, I think I'm going to bed he texted.

I might. I fell asleep right after coming home from school.

So you're still grounded till Monday?

If I behave well, yeah.

All right. Text me later.

I put my phone in one of my dresser drawers, so I wouldn't be tempted to scroll through it and waste more time being awake. Eventually, the temptation proved to be stronger and I grabbed my phone back and Googled Gladys' name. The first article that came up was about the Corpus Christi sighting. There was a picture to go along with the story. It was blurry and the woman in the picture had big sunglasses on, so it was hard to tell if it was her or not. Whether it was or not, the picture gave Lalo a glimmer of hope and did the same for me. There hadn't been anything in the news suggesting Gladys was dead. Most likely, she was alive somewhere. I shoved my phone away and managed to sleep a few more hours until I heard Aunt Sazón cooking breakfast.

For breakfast, Aunt Sazón boiled eggs for me and Uncle Pico, which I hated. I hated their feel, smell, and taste. But since there wasn't anything else, I swallowed mine in two halves. Uncle Pico slammed his fist on the kitchen table when Aunt Sazón served him. "This is it? I'm supposed to eat this?"

"I'm exhausted," Aunt Sazón said. "If you want something else, you can cook it."

Uncle Pico stayed silent. It was the first time in my whole life I'd heard Aunt Sazón tell him off. It was odd, yet amazing.

"What?" he said. "I don't know how to cook."

"You're a grown man," she said. "It's time you learned."

I watched Uncle Pico's eyes widen and his mouth drop. "But," he said, stammering. "I have *you*."

"Pico…" she said with a long groan. "I'm exhausted."

"From what?"

"Everything."

Instead of talking more, Uncle Pico took his egg, tossed it in the trash can, and left without a word. I wanted him to come back in and say "Let me tell you one more thing!" so I could watch the drama unfold, but he didn't. I was surprised to hear Aunt Sazón speak to him that way. She'd talk smack to everyone else, but never to Uncle Pico, Uncle Juke, or my cousins.

"Everything okay?" I asked to break the silence.

"I'm tired. I've been doing everything for so long. I need a break."

"Take one. Don't worry about me. I can stay with Lalo or Brandon."

"Not a chance," she said, even though Ajo and Oregano spent the night at their girlfriends' houses whenever they wanted. "I'm not letting you stay with a boy."

Since Aunt Sazón needed time to herself, she told me I wasn't grounded anymore, but I had to be home by six or she'd send Uncle Juke to find me. I took off to Lalo's, thinking he'd be up to do something, but he wasn't.

"Stupid chili," he said, clutching his stomach. "I think my mom put a bad pepper in it."

"You ate chili for breakfast? You're gonna be blasting farts until next week."

"Mom and Dad still haven't gone to the store. It was either leftover chili or expired cereal. Weren't you supposed to hang out with Tiana today anyway?"

"Oh crap. I totally forgot."

"She texted me earlier saying she couldn't get ahold of you, but I told her you were grounded. If you want, you can pretend you still are."

"I dunno. She's nice."

"She's very…" he said, holding his stomach. "Loud? I think she's nice, too, but sometimes she needs to take her voice down a notch."

"It's fine. I'll hang out with her. I hope you feel better."

"Me too. I got enough gas to start my own station."

I said bye to Lalo and texted Tiana as I headed to Brandon's. She texted back right away, which disappointed me.

Awesome! Can we meet up at Retro World at 3?

Yeah, I'll be there.

See you later!

When I got to Brandon's, he was out on his lawn, cutting the grass.

"Home alone?" I asked him through the noise of the lawnmower.

"Nope," he said, shutting off the lawnmower. "Dad asked me to chop the grass up. He's sleeping. He came home at five in the morning."

"Lots of work last night?"

"Oh yeah," Brandon answered, wiping his forehead with his hand. "He broke up a couple fights. He got scratched, but he's fine."

"Good, I'm glad. I'm hanging out with Tiana later."

"She's all right," he said. "Her friend Nate gives me the creeps though."

"What? Why?"

"Something about his eyes. He looks like he's afraid of me."

"You scared him with your serial killer talk."

"What a wuss."

When I was about to take off, Mr. Meyer stepped outside in a blue robe and battered slippers. His beard was sprawled, like it was trying to escape from his round face.

"Hi Elysian!" Mr. Meyer said. "How you doing?"

"All right, I guess."

"You going somewhere?"

"Library to chill out for a bit," I said.

"I'll take you, I'm headed to the grocery store."

I thought Brandon would come with us, but he stayed home to finish cutting the grass since he still had to do the backyard. Mr. Meyer drove slower than usual thanks to new construction detours. His car reeked of cigarette smoke and strong cologne. I noticed a deep scratch on his right arm and another on his right cheek. He pulled out his pack of cigarettes from his pocket. He lit one up at the next red light and cracked his window open to let the smoke out.

"How's school?" he asked.

"Fine. How's work?"

"Eh, it's work. Brandon might've told you I had to stop a couple of fights last night. One of the security guards is on vacation. Drunk dudes love to start shit."

"Do you ever think about getting another job? Like one with regular hours during the day?"

"Of course I do. But I don't have much education, so I don't have many choices. I've thought about going back to school during the day, but when I get off from work, I'm so tired I can sleep for a century."

Every time I was around Mr. Meyer, I couldn't believe he was a bouncer. Years ago, he had been a Hasidic Jew. He grew up in a close-knit Hasidic community in New York City where he rarely left his neighborhood. He went to a Jewish school, studied the Torah intensely, prayed often, and went to the synagogue every single day.

I didn't believe anything about his past life until Mr. Meyer showed me a picture of himself from when he was fifteen. He had long locks of hair, a black hat, and a long, black coat. "That was me," he said when he showed me the picture. "Don't I look stupid?"

"No, just different."

It was very hard for me to imagine a big, tough guy bouncer like Mr. Meyer used to be so religious, he would only eat foods that were prepared a certain way. Now, he ate whatever he wanted, smoked, drank, cursed, and worked at a nightclub.

"Mr. Meyer, how come you left the Hasidic thing anyway? You never told me."

"Simple. Wasn't for me."

"What was wrong with it?"

"Nothing particularly. It's not a bad place, it's just not for everyone, you know? Some people are truly happy there. It's like the library I'm taking you to. Library ain't a bad spot, but not everyone likes to read. I hate the idea that you have to live a certain way or you're wrong. Screw that! If I want to eat ham, I should be able to eat the whole pig!"

"I thought it was the religion itself, not the eating ham thing?"

"It is," he said. "Makes no sense to me. Why would God make

all these animals and then tell you only a select group of them can be eaten?"

"Hmm. Good point."

"Isn't it?" Mr. Meyer said, puffing thick smoke out the window. "But if you bring up those kinds of questions to the Hasidic community like the one I grew up in, you're treated like you don't belong. I got sick of it. Right before my arranged wedding to a woman I didn't know, I took off. I packed a bag and left while my parents and my siblings slept. For a while, I lived on the streets. Then I got a job at a little sex shop in Manhattan. Boy, was I confused! I didn't even know what the hell sex was!"

"Do you ever think about rejoining?"

"I used to," he said. "During my first year away, I got homesick. I missed my family, I missed my daily routine, I missed my rabbi. But they would never take me back. I don't exist to them anymore. It's not like I'm dead to them. They just act like I don't exist. Like I *never* existed. Like I'm some kind of myth... but I'm actually here, living and breathing."

Mr. Meyer dropped me off at the library's side entrance. I thanked him for the ride and he sped down Crockett Boulevard. I didn't go to the library often since there were tons of books at home, plus I got to use Mom and Dad's professor accounts to check out eBooks from Saint Jerome's library. Rey Carlos Island Library wasn't the greatest. During the last few hurricanes we had, it flooded and repairs were barely done. Each time I went, the library looked worse than before and their collection of books got smaller and smaller. They had computers, but only half of them worked. I found a computer that did and went online to check my emails. Mom had written me one and included pictures. She had recently given a lecture at a library in Buenos Aires. The audience was packed with people who looked excited to hear

Mom speak about her anthropology theories. I was proud of her, but I missed her a lot. I wasn't looking forward to her coming home because I knew she and Dad would be invited to another teaching fellowship and they'd leave again. They never refused any offers, but I wished they would start.

After the library, I started the walk to Retro World. Tiana was already there, playing a game on her phone and wearing enough makeup to try out for the circus.

"Eh-lee-shun!" she said.

"Hey," I said, scrunching up my nose at the mispronunciation of my name.

"So glad you're not grounded! We're gonna have such a great girl's day out."

"Oh yeah. Such a great day."

Tiana ordered us a platter of mixed appetizers – mozzarella sticks, hot wings, fried pickle slices, and hush puppies. While we ate, she talked to me about everything from books she read for Book Club to how cute Brandon was when he talked about true crime. Sometimes she spoke way too fast, but I got used to it after a while.

"You're quiet," she said. "What's up?"

"Nothing."

"What did you do this morning?"

"I hung out at the library."

"Fancy! Why don't you join Book Club?" she asked, biting into a fried pickle slice.

"I don't like clubbing."

"Silly! It's not *that* kind of club!" she said.

"I'll think about it," I said, even though I wouldn't.

"We need sodas," she said, raising her hand to our server. "Two sodas, please. I'll have the orange. What do you want,

Eh-lee-shun?”

"Lemon," I said to our server. I wanted to address her by name, but her nametag was faded. "Light on the ice, please."

"You got it, doll," the server said and walked away.

The moment she came back with our sodas, Octavio walked in, ready for his shift. His eyes were redder than fresh strawberries. He walked past our booth, but I called out his name to make him stop.

"Oh, hey," he said, tugging at his shirt collar. "Heard anything?"

"Nope."

"Who's this, Eh-lee-shun?" Tiana asked. "He's cute!"

"This is Octavio, Gladys' husband."

"I'm sorry," Tiana told him. "I'm sure she's fine."

"Hopefully," he answered with sweat coming down from his forehead. "Well, I have to get to work. Have a good lunch." He adjusted his cap and quickly walked through the swinging doors that led to the kitchen.

"What's next?" Tiana asked. "Beach?"

"No!" I said, loud enough for the other people inside Retro World to turn around and look at me. "Not there. It's supposed to rain today, I think."

"Today? My phone says there's only a twenty percent chance. C'mon, it'll be fun! We can go to Jasper's for ice cream."

"I don't want ice cream."

"Eh-lee-shun, it's just the beach. We're islanders, the beach is all we have."

"Fine," I said. "Just Jasper's."

"Sure, whatever you want," she said, throwing cash on the table.

We walked out of Retro World and headed down Seashore Lane.

From there, it was a one-mile walk to Emerald Beach. I couldn't believe Tiana picked the beach. *Did she forget what happened the last time we went to the beach? Wasn't she scared it could happen again? Did she think about wearing a bulletproof vest? Why the hell would she return to the place where she almost got killed? What was wrong with her?*

"It's so hot," she said. "So, so, so hot."

"Always is."

"Maybe we'll have a cold front this year."

"Who knows?" I said, feeling my heart race as we got closer to Emerald Beach.

"Mr. Jasper makes the best vanilla ice cream. I think I'll get a scoop of it with sprinkles. What about you?"

"Uh, I'll probably get the same."

The line for Jasper's was long as usual. We stood there, waiting for our turn. Tiana yakked and yakked and I tuned her out by humming in my head. After standing in the sun for a decade, Mr. Jasper finally called us up.

"Best ice cream on the island," he said in his hoarse voice. "What are we having?"

"Vanilla, one scoop!" Tiana answered. "Chocolate sprinkles, please!"

"And you, Elysian?" Mr. Jasper asked, pronouncing my name correctly.

"Coconut," I said. "One scoop, no toppings."

"You got it!" he said. "Six dollars!"

As we waited for Mr. Jasper to make our scoops, we stepped aside and stood close to the stairwell leading to the beach's sand. Kids ran around flying kites, others built sandcastles, and some played with beach balls. I couldn't believe their parents brought them to Emerald Beach after what had happened.

"Order 38!" I heard Mr. Jasper shout. Tiana went to the pick-up window to get our scoops. She handed me a spoon and we started eating. She yakked about something else, but I didn't hear what. Three bites into my ice cream, I got weak-kneed and sat on one of the stairwell steps. My lungs felt like they were going to blow up. Tiana stopped eating and asked what was wrong.

"I need to get out of here," I told her. "Now."

"Can you walk?"

"I don't know," I said. Tears fell from my eyes and into my melting ice cream. She tried to help me stand, but I couldn't budge. She called Lalo and put him on speakerphone the second he picked up.

"She's freaked out about something," Tiana said. "I don't know what to do."

"Elysian?" Lalo said. "Leave the beach and come over."

"I can't walk," I answered. "Can't breathe."

"Do you need to go to the hospital?" Tiana asked.

"Yes," I said. "Call 911."

Within minutes, paramedics arrived and strapped me to a stretcher before placing me inside the ambulance. Tiana rode with me, texting Lalo and Brandon with updates the entire way. This panic attack felt different than the others. Usually, I was able to calm down, but this one just wouldn't stop. We arrived at the hospital and I was immediately taken to a room to wait for a doctor.

Tiana stood at the foot of my hospital bed, texting nonstop. "Do you want me to call your aunt? Or your uncle?"

"Oh God no," I answered.

"Then who?"

"Brandon's dad."

"What? Why?"

"Please," I said with strong wheezing.

She left the room for twenty minutes and came back with a cold bottle of water for me. "I called Mr. Meyer. He should be here soon. He told me to buy you some water. Why did you want me to call him?"

"He's funny," I said. "He can help me calm down."

Mr. Meyer arrived with Brandon and Lalo almost an hour later. A doctor still hadn't seen me yet. The rules for the emergency room area were two visitors maximum, so Tiana and Lalo stepped out to let Mr. Meyer and Brandon visit with me.

"You're in luck today," Mr. Meyer said, holding up a big backpack. "I brought props!"

"Dad, what?" Brandon groaned.

"Boy, let me put on my show," Mr. Meyer answered. "You're lucky I ain't charging a cover price. Step aside and let me start."

He unzipped the backpack, pulled out a giant cowboy hat and changed his voice to a deep, Southern drawl. "Hey there, Elysian, I'm Cowboy Cal! My favorite things to do are eat barbecue, ride my horse... and my cousins."

"Dad! That is messed up!" Brandon said.

"You don't like my act? What's wrong with my act? Do you like my act, Elysian?"

"I just want to feel better," I said, taking a sip of cold water.

"I've got it... a Hasidic act!"

"Uhm," I said. "Okay?"

Mr. Meyer grabbed a surgical mask from a dispenser by my bed and placed it on his head, before changing his voice to another accent. He told me he was Rabbi M and said I was due to marry the village idiot.

"Who's the village idiot?" I asked.

"Brandon Meyer!"

"Jesus Christ, Dad," Brandon said, covering his face with his right hand. "This is awful."

"Who is Christ? I'm Jewish, you *nebbish*."

When the doctor finally walked inside my room, she introduced herself as Dr. Patricia Lara before turning to Brandon and Mr. Meyer. "Is the show over or is there an encore?"

"Nah, shit show's done," Brandon said as Mr. Meyer waved a fist at him.

"Your vitals are back to normal," Dr. Lara told me. "Labs are good, too. We checked your bloodwork and your urine sample. Nothing is wrong."

"Why do I feel like something's wrong?"

"Well, nothing is physically wrong with you," she said, using her cold stethoscope to check my heart and lungs. "You have anxiety."

"Anxiety?"

"It's common," Dr. Lara said, using her otoscope to look into my ears. "Many people have anxiety. We'll give you a few pamphlets for you to read more about it."

"So, she's okay, Dr. Lara?" Mr. Meyer asked.

"She's fine. I don't know if I can say the same for you though, sir," Dr. Lara said, making me laugh a real laugh for the first time the entire day. "I'm discharging her. Take her home, let her rest."

The discharge took another half hour. When I was out at last, I held the anxiety pamphlets tightly in my hands as we all squeezed into Mr. Meyer's car.

"Tiana, where do you live?" Mr. Meyer asked her.

"297 Gonzalez Street."

"Lalo?" he asked.

"8965 Waterstone, Mr. Meyer. Down the street from Elysian."

"How about you, Brandon?"

"C'mon Dad," he said. "You know where I live."

"Sure do," Mr. Meyer said. "123 *Nebbish* Avenue."

Mr. Meyer dropped off Tiana first and then took Lalo home. When we got to my house, nobody was there. I called Aunt Sazón and she told me she'd gone shopping with Canelo. She wouldn't be done for at least another two hours.

"Where should I go then?" I asked her.

"Stay home. I'll tell Uncle Juke to stop by."

"Can't I stick with Brandon or Lalo?"

"Ella," she said. "You're a girl, you can't stay with boys."

Mr. Meyer and Brandon walked me inside. They served me cold water and asked if I needed or wanted anything else. I wanted them to stay with me for a while, but I didn't want to hear more "you're a girl" crap from Aunt Sazón.

"My uncle will be here soon. I'll see you guys later. Thanks for coming to my rescue. Mr. Meyer, you're a much better bouncer than comedian. Sorry."

"Hey, that's why I am a bouncer," he said. "Don't hurt yourself, okay? Anxiety's a bitch, but you can take it."

"I'll text you later, Elysian," Brandon said. "See ya."

They stepped outside and I heard Mr. Meyer switch on his car and yell out, "Damn it, Brandon! I still had the surgical mask on my head and you didn't tell me?"

My house grew quiet again. Uncle Juke texted me a second time to tell me he'd be over a little later since he had stopped to get dinner at Groovy Burger, a new joint not far from our neighborhood. He asked me if I wanted anything, but I said no.

I flipped on the TV to drown out the overwhelming silence.

The news was on, talking about burglaries, assaults, murders, and hate crimes, so I changed the channel to a game show.

As the host asked questions, I read the anxiety pamphlets. They said the condition was common and nothing to feel ashamed about. The typical symptoms were worrying, panic attacks, endless fears, trouble sleeping, and a lot more. It wasn't me being weird. None of the emotions or attacks were my fault. It was anxiety. I had finally found out what was wrong with me, and for some reason, knowing the answer made me feel normal.

"Your best uncle's here," Uncle Juke announced, walking in with a greasy paper bag in his arm. "Groovy Burger was packed as hell. What are you doing watching TV? Don't you have homework?"

"No."

"What are you reading?" he asked, taking a sip of his soda.

"Oh, I got these at the library."

"Let me see," he said, sticking out his dirty hand. I gave the pamphlets to him and he skimmed through each one, laughing as he read. "They found a name for being a wuss? Scientists research the dumbest dirt."

"I don't think that's what anxiety is. Those pamphlets say it can be serious."

"This is a bunch of nonsense. Anxiety doesn't exist in Ecuador."

"What?"

"No one has it there. That's an American thing," he said, reaching into his greasy bag and pulling out a few French fries. "Anxiety isn't real."

Chapter 11

I didn't break my silence about the ER visit to Aunt Sazón until a week later.

"I can't believe this!" she said, with her eyes bulging. "You went to the ER and didn't say *anything*?!"

"I didn't want to. I wasn't thinking right. The pamphlets the doctor gave me say anxiety can clog up your thinking."

"You can't possibly think anxiety is real. You're a teenager—of course you're worried about the future. What you have isn't anxiety… it's just everyday worries." She told me I should try making more friends, learn how to sew, learn how to cook, or other hobbies like those to keep my mind busy. What she didn't understand was how busy my mind was all the time. I couldn't get it to shut up. It was like trying to turn off a blaring TV in the middle of the night, but the TV would keep playing even after you pressed the OFF button.

"If you pick up new hobbies, you'll be fine," Aunt Sazón assured me. "I promise. Anxiety is not real, Ella."

Later that day, I went to Lalo's. To my surprise, his parents were home. Mr. Richardson had taken a sick day from his business and Mrs. Richardson was taking care of him. He coughed and sneezed so loud, I heard it from Lalo's living room.

"Hey," I said to Lalo. "Anything about Gladys?"

"Yep, another sighting."

"Where?"

"Corpus Christi again. How's your aunt?"

"I dunno, she's around. She can still talk unfortunately."

"That sucks to hear," he said. "You have my deepest condolences. May the Lord be with you during this hard time."

"Thanks, Lalo. Do you wanna hang out somewhere?"

"I just wanna stay home today. Tiana might wanna see you though."

"Shut up, Lalo."

"Elysian and Tiana sitting in a boat... Elysian jumped off and hit the moat."

"What?! Why did I hit the moat?"

"Because you jumped out of the boat!"

"There is no boat!"

"Whatever Elysian, go push people," he said, laughing. I had never noticed how cute he was when he laughed.

"I guess I'm gonna go to the library or something. I'll text you later. Bye Mr. R! Bye Mrs. R!"

"Bye Elysian!" Mr. Richardson answered with a cough.

"Bye Elysian!" Mrs. Richardson said. "Be careful out there. Call us if you need anything. Tell your aunt we said hi."

Lalo walked me outside. Younger kids from the neighborhood sped past us on their bikes, singing the infamous "sitting in a tree" song when they saw us standing together.

"You know what, Elysian?" he said after the kids were gone. "I think Gladys is dead."

"You don't know for sure," I told him, even though my anxious mind screamed, *Of course she's dead, you idiot!*

"It's been a long time. There's no way she's alive. I haven't talked to my parents about it, but they probably think the same.

Anyway, text me later, okay?"

"I will. Bye Lalo."

"See ya," he said. "Don't push any old ladies at the library."

The library was extra quiet when I got there. I counted four people in the computer lab and two in the reading lounge. The librarians were at their desks, reading older copies of *Reader's Digest*. One of them asked if I needed any help finding something, but I told them I was only browsing.

I took the elevator to the fourth floor where the history books and artifacts were. There was a mural on the left wall, painted when I was first grade or so, explaining the history of Rey Carlos Island. It talked about how a Spanish conquistador named Diego Madrazo discovered the island in 1689 and immediately named it La Isla de Rey Carlos. The inhabitants were Native Americans who thought it was messed up that some random dude renamed their island after a king they had never heard of, so they went to battle with the conquistadors right away. Within a month, Madrazo and his men murdered nearly the whole tribe. After that, Rey Carlos Island belonged to Spain, then Mexico, and then Texas. I felt sorry for the Native Americans who lived on the island. I couldn't imagine minding my own business, just for some guy to walk in and scream that my house was his house. It sounded pretty ridiculous, but it happened a lot throughout history.

After I finished reading about Rey Carlos Island's background, I took a seat by the center window and looked out at Emerald Beach. I could see the USS Defiance. From what I knew, it was struck by kamikazes and torpedoed several times. I wished I could be like the USS Defiance: terrorized by fears, worries, and panic attacks, but still strong.

"She's a beauty, isn't she?" an older man told me as he

pointed to the USS Defiance. "My father fought like hell from her walls. Hit by kamikazes, but there she is. You ever taken a field trip there?"

"Oh yeah," I said. "Tons of times."

"You'll learn something new each time you go," he said, starting to walk off. "She's what makes our island beautiful."

I left the library around 2:30 in the afternoon and headed to the USS Defiance. I knew I had to go through Emerald Beach to get there, but in that moment, I felt like I actually could. During the walk, my muscles tensed. My breathing increased, my heart pounded, but I kept walking. By the time I reached the USS Defiance, I thought I'd tumble over the dock and crush my head on the rocks below before plunging into the ocean.

"One ticket?" the entrance attendant asked me. "Child?"

"I'm fourteen," I said.

"It's okay, take a kid's ticket. It's cheaper. Eight bucks."

I paid the eight dollars using crumpled bills. She pressed a button on top of her desk to allow the turnstile to let me in. The first area I checked out was the Defiance Deli. I checked my wallet and saw I only had a five-dollar bill left. The fish and fries meal looked good, but I settled for the half turkey sandwich and bag of chips. I didn't have enough money for a drink, so I ran back and forth to the water fountain as I ate.

When I was done, I started the self-tour. The signs around the USS Defiance showed exactly where to start and places that couldn't be entered, because they were private or under construction for a new exhibit. It had been a couple years since I was last inside. I couldn't remember whether it was a field trip or with Mom and Dad. Some evenings, the USS Defiance held private events like weddings, charity fundraisers, and academic events. Mom and Dad had spoken at the USS Defiance several times. Last time they did, I didn't go because I didn't feel like leaving the house. I should've gone, though. It's not like I got to spend much time with them anyway.

At the middle of the tour, I got to my favorite part. There was a mini-hospital complete with an eye doctor's office, a dentist, and a surgery room. There were dummies all over the warship resembling sailors, captains, and other employees to make it look the way it did back in World War II. The dental office, on the other hand, had sound effects. Inside, there was a dentist dummy who looked straight from hell who was drilling into a patient dummy's teeth. You could hear the drill spins followed by "Ouch, my gosh darn it, dagnabbit aching tooth!" about a hundred times in a row. The recording was incredibly unrealistic for a sailor's vocabulary and it made me laugh out loud every time I heard it. As I stood by the dental office laughing to myself, Lalo texted me.

Where are you?

USS Defiance.

Whaaaaaaaat? Why?

I dunno, felt like checking it out.

Sweet. Have fun. Call me when you get home.

I tried to text back, but lost signal the second I stepped out of the dental office. The next part of the exhibit was the surgery room, the coldest room of them all. There were enormous vents in the ceiling, letting out freezing air every second. The surgery room didn't have any sound effects, but it had tons of exhibit pieces like old scalpels, scissors, and stitch thread. I tried looking at all the pieces, but the arctic air was too much.

The final part of the tour was the chapel. It had several rows of pews, a podium, stained glass windows, and shelves with old Bibles, Torahs, Qurans, Vedas, and other religious books.

There was a glass case that held rosaries, prayer shawls, prayer rugs, and cross necklaces which once belonged to the sailors. According to an information panel, most of the USS Defiance veterans were dead. If they weren't yet, they would be soon. Another panel inside the chapel said a total of 557 men died while fighting onboard. I wondered what was in their heads when they knew their time was up. *Did they pray? Did they hide? Did they think about abandoning the ship? Did they say something along the lines of "gosh darn it, dagnabbit, the enemy's here?"* Whatever they thought, I was sure they were way braver than me. I was one hundred percent certain none of them had anxiety. I could barely live through normal, daily life. There was no way in hell I could've been on the USS Defiance.

"Thank you for visiting," the guard said at the exit. "Come back and sail with us again."

I walked outside and my phone buzzed with text and call notifications when I got signal back. Aunt Sazón had called me six times, texted twice, and left three voicemails. When I reached the end of the dock, I listened to one of the voicemails.

"Where the heck are you? Lalo, Brandon, and Tiana are on TV! The cops found the shooter. If you don't call me within the next hour, I'm going to call the police."

Instead of walking home, I ran. My feet ached, but I kept moving until I arrived at the entrance of my neighborhood. News vans were in front of Lalo's house. Photographers snapped pictures of him, Brandon, and Tiana. One of the journalists asked Lalo how he felt to be alive.

"It's not great," he said. "My sister is still missing. Her name is Gladys Richardson, she's twenty-two, she speaks English and Spanish. She has a birthmark on her left cheek that looks like a butterfly. If anyone has seen her, please tell the police. I won't feel great about being alive until I know what happened to my big sister."

When the news vans left, I hung out with Lalo, Brandon, and Tiana inside Lalo's house. Mrs. Richardson ordered Chinese takeout for us. She'd check on us periodically and then head back to the bedroom to check on Mr. Richardson.

"I can't believe they got the son of a bitch!" Brandon said, chewing on a piece of a fortune cookie. "Amazing!"

"Who was it?" I asked.

"A thirty-year-old named Mark Pilsner," Tiana said. "No previous records or anything, but the cops think he was paid to do it. He's the photographer from Austin that Gladys planned to meet up with."

"Well, he did a shitty job. The doofus didn't even kill anyone," Brandon said, breaking another fortune cookie in two. "Great fortune I got: *'do all things carefully.'* Yeah man, don't run with scissors either."

"He couldn't have done it," Lalo said. "Why would he? Why would he drive all the way down to this island to shoot up the beach? It makes no sense."

"You think he didn't do it?" Tiana asked. "The cops don't arrest people for no reason."

"I'm gonna head home," I said, standing up from my seat.

"Take some food with you if you want," Lalo said. He offered me a full box of fried rice and two fortune cookies, but I turned it down. I said bye to him, Brandon, and Tiana and walked outside. The sun was already setting, so I walked quickly.

When I got home, Uncle Pico was there, sitting on the couch and watching the evening news. "Where the hell have you been?"

"I went to the library. And the USS Defiance. Then, I went to

Lalo's house."

"You better start learning how to communicate," he said, shutting off the TV. "You think girls can go out without telling anyone?"

"I'm sorry. I meant to call, but I forgot."

"Go wash up. Your aunt went home to help Canelo with homework, but she'll be back soon. You better behave."

I drew myself a bubble bath. While I waited for the water to warm up, I looked up articles on my phone about Mark Pilsner. Some of them said he was a lone wolf; others said there was suspicion he had one or more partners. But, why would he shoot random people at Emerald Beach? Did he purposely shoot people in areas where they wouldn't bleed to death? He was a photographer from Austin with a pretty solid career from what the article said. He had no prior records either. From what I read, he didn't have a motive. It seemed unbelievable.

At last, the water was warm enough for me to get in. I shoved my phone away in one of the sink drawers and eased down into the tub. The bubbles smelled minty, a little too strong at first, but I got used to the scent after a while. I closed my eyes as the water seeped over me.

I pictured myself in a world where nothing was wrong. Gladys was back home, Mom and Dad stopped going on teaching fellowships, Brandon's parents were together again, Tiana and I were friends, and Lalo's parents worked regular schedules. As for me, my family didn't criticize me anymore. They accepted me and considered me part of the family.

But when I opened my eyes, I remembered everything.

Chapter 12

Madrazo Middle School was the only middle school in the whole district that gave midterms and they were coming soon. Brandon and I met up at the Rey Carlos Island Library to study for our geology midterm.

"Rocks, rocks, rocks," he said. "Who gets this?"

"Mr. Garrison."

"Mr. Garrison needs a new hobby."

"Geology's way easier than biology would have been. No dissections either."

"I wouldn't mind dissecting something. It'd be more interesting than looking at rocks."

"What did you get for question four? It says what kind of rock is granite?"

"Igneous," he answered, cracking his knuckles.

"Really?"

"That's what the book says, but there's no way I'm gonna remember all the different types. When am I gonna use this stuff anyway?"

"If you ever trip on a rock, you'll know what kind it is."

After we studied for about two hours, we left the library and walked to Prince Griddle's in time for the lunch special. We got plates of tacos, beans, and rice for four dollars each.

"When's our test again?" Brandon asked.

"Monday."

"I think I'm going to skip."

"You can't skip, you'll have to make it up anyway."

"Bingo!" he said. "More time to study."

"Hey Brandon," I said, taking a sip of lemonade. "This is a weird question, but do you think your dad would ever go back to being Hasidic?"

"Nope, never," he said, passing me the salsa for my tacos. "I mean, it's a lifestyle, you know? I just wish I could meet my grandparents."

"You've never met your grandparents?"

"My mom's parents. My dad's parents disowned him when he left. They know I exist, but they don't acknowledge my existence. Isn't that a bitch?"

"Wow. Why would they do that to you?"

"Eh," he said, shrugging his shoulders. "I get it. They live in a way that's closed off and anything that's different is seen as a threat. Like the Amish or whatever. I might not like it, but I get it. I'd like to meet them someday. Maybe I'll go undercover and pretend to be a stranger who wants to join them."

"Yeah, that'd be pretty cool."

"I wouldn't last. Five minutes in there and I'd cuss at someone."

After lunch, Brandon and I went to his house to compare our study guides one more time. Mr. Meyer was there, kicking back on his couch with an open bag of chips in his right hand and a large, fresh scratch across his left cheek.

"Another fight," he said when he noticed me looking. "Another fight, another dollar. Clubbers!"

"Dad, don't fight them, call the cops," Brandon said. "You

might get hurt someday if you keep getting in their faces."

"They don't scare me. I can take them."

After Brandon and I finished looking over our notes, Mr. Meyer offered to drive me home, so Brandon came along with us. In the car, Mr. Meyer flipped on the radio to the classic rock station and sped towards my neighborhood.

"I'm happy the cops finally found the son of a bitch who shot Brandon," Mr. Meyer said over the music.

"I wonder why he did it," I said. "He had no reason to."

"Paid off! If someone paid me a bunch of money, I'd do a hell of a lot of things. I wonder how much he was bought for."

"I'm guessing at least ten grand," Brandon said.

"Sounds about right," Mr. Meyer agreed. "I'm glad he's behind bars now. If I had the chance, I'd beat the sucker just enough to scare him."

When we got to my house, I saw Canelo running around the front lawn. Aunt Sazón was behind him, telling him to get inside and put on sunscreen.

"Mama, I'm fi-iiine!" he said.

"Damn," Mr. Meyer said, witnessing the absurdity of my youngest cousin. "That little guy's related to you, Elysian?"

"Unfortunately," I said, opening the car door to let myself out. "He's not the worst relative I have, just the whiniest."

"I'll text you later, Elysian," Brandon told me.

"See ya. Thanks for the ride, Mr. Meyer."

"You got it," he said, reversing his car out of the driveway. I walked up to Aunt Sazón and saw her face turn redder and redder as Canelo continued running around.

"This boy doesn't listen to me," she said with a sigh. "Why is he so difficult?"

"CANELO!" I yelled, causing him to stop and turn his head to look at me. "Quit running around! Your mom said you need to wear sunscreen!"

"You can't make me!"

"All right, stay out here and burn to death. That's how Grandpa died. He stood outside without sunscreen and when Grandma went to check on him, he was ashes."

Canelo instantly rushed inside my house as Aunt Sazón squinted her eyes at me and shook her head several times.

"How could you scare him like that? He's sensitive!"

"He listened, didn't he?"

While Aunt Sazón made dinner, she kept her eyes on Canelo. He was out playing in the backyard, appearing dirtier and dirtier every time I looked at him. When he toppled over and hurt his knee, he ran inside crying so hard, I thought he had broken every bone in his body.

"You're okay," I told him. "Follow me to the bathroom, I'll fix you up."

"I'm gonna burn up like Grandpa!"

"Keep yelling like that and you will. Let's go."

In the bathroom, Canelo sat down on the toilet. I took out the first aid kit, cleaned his cut with rubbing alcohol, listened to him shriek, and placed fresh gauze over the blood while I took out a band aid. I told him to count backwards from ten as a distraction as I placed the band aid on his knee, but he wouldn't stop screaming.

"Canelo! What's wrong?"

"It hurts!"

"Does it really hurt that much? It's not bad."

"It's not?" he asked. "Are you sure?"

"The cut is super tiny."

"Oh. Then, I guess I'm okay."

"Seriously? You were screaming your head off and you're fine?"

"If I scream enough, my mom will give me ice cream so I can feel better," he whispered.

"Canelo, you can leave now," I said. He stood up from the toilet and ran down the hallway, his feet slamming against the floor.

After dinner, Mom and Dad videocalled me. They were inside their spacious dorm room, provided by the university. Dad showed me every inch, even the bathroom. "Look at the toilet, Elysian! So clean, I'd eat off it!"

"Would you give me the phone back?" I heard Mom say just before she came on camera. "This is a great dorm, the best one we've ever had. We miss you, Elysian. How is school? How is everyone back home?"

"Oh, fine."

"Are you feeling okay?"

I didn't know why she wanted to know. I hadn't told her or Dad about my anxiety diagnosis. Dad, with his biology professor mind, would want to study my behavior. I pictured him following me around, writing notes, and asking me interview questions, so he'd have enough material to write another textbook. Mom would research anxiety of the past and tell me to look at the skulls of *homo habilis* or whatever she thought was good to study. They had knowledge, but emotional support wasn't one of their fields.

"Yeah," I said. "I'm fine. The person who shot up the beach was caught."

"Yes! Aunt Sazón emailed us an article about it. We're happy to hear he's in custody. Here, sweetie, your dad wants to say goodnight."

"Elysian," he said, smiling. "My best girl. Are you making straight A's?"

"Of course I am."

"That's what I like to hear. One day you might be a professor like your mother and I. You'll travel the world teaching what you know best."

"Right, Dad. I'd love to be a professor like you and Mom."

"Well, we're going to get ready for bed," Dad said. "Goodnight, sweetie. If Uncle Juke bothers you too much, kick him in the groin."

"I will, Dad."

"Goodnight, Elysian," Mom said. "My heavenly daughter."

They waved to me through the camera and signed out. There were two more months to go until I'd see them in person again.

Chapter 13

On Monday morning, midterms were put on hold. Principal Jarmon came on the intercom and announced a lockdown. I thought it was a drill at first, but it wasn't. Ms. Bautista barricaded the classroom door with several chairs, turned off the lights, and told us to be quiet. I crawled underneath my desk as Lalo shivered next to me.

"What do you think is happening?" he whispered.

"I don't know," I said, trying to hold myself together. My skin broke out into a sweat, my teeth chattered, and my breathing escalated. I worried whoever was outside would find us and take us hostage or kill us. Since I had to keep quiet, I closed my eyes tightly. I took a deep breath and repeated the quadratic formula in my head.

After what felt like hours, Principal Jarmon finally came in over the intercom. "You may resume classes. All is clear."

"I wonder what that was about," Lalo said.

"Okay class, back to your seats," Ms. Bautista said. "Get out your pencils. Test time!"

The test wasn't as hard as I thought. Lalo, on the other hand, was sweating so much, his desk had a puddle by the time he finished. When the last classmate turned in her test, we were allowed to talk quietly until the bell rang.

"Man," Lalo said. "That was *hard*."

"I didn't think it was. Could have been harder."

"Any harder and my head would've exploded."

"Eww, then your brain guts would be everywhere."

"Brain guts, brain guts, brain guts," he said, dancing in his chair.

At lunch, we sat with Brandon, Tiana, and Nate as usual. Nate shakily drank a carton of chocolate milk and ate carrot sticks.

"Are you all right, Nate?" I asked.

"I'm worried about my biology midterm."

"What's there to biology?" Brandon asked. "The head bone's connected to the neck bone. Try learning about rocks."

"Hey Elysian," Tiana said. "Wanna hang out with me after school?" Before I could make up an excuse, she quickly followed up. "Great! Let's go to my parents' bakery. We can eat for free."

"I'm tired," Lalo said, patting his forehead with a napkin. "That math test was intense. I wonder why people go to college and choose to major in math. They must be really, really smart or really, really dumb."

"If they were dumb, they wouldn't major in math, you dork," Brandon said.

"Do you know how hard it must be to major in math?" Lalo said. "If you're smart, you should major in something easy... like Underwater Spanish."

"What's Underwater Spanish?" Brandon asked. "Do you put on a snorkel and say *hola* to all the fish?"'

Lalo, Tiana, Nate, and I laughed as the bell rang and we got up to face two more midterms. I had English and history left, but they were my stronger subjects. Before going to Ms. Ochoa's class, I stopped by my locker for a minute to grab extra pencils. To my luck, the box they were in flew out and crashed on the floor. By the time I picked up the mess, the tardy bell had already rang.

"Elysian, you're late," Ms. Ochoa said when I walked in. "Go to the office and get a tardy slip."

"If I do that, I'll be even more late."

"Don't argue with me, you know the rules," she said, holding up her big glasses with her right hand. "If you need more time for your test, you can always stay after school."

I left the classroom and took the long stairwell down to the first floor. When the office staff asked why I was late, I told one of the receptionists what happened to my pencil box.

"You really expect me to believe you were late because you wanted extra pencils?" Mr. Kingston asked. "If you're going to lie, at least make up something believable."

"I'm not lying. Go ahead, check the camera footage if you want."

"You think I have time to check camera footage?"

"You have time to tell me I'm lying, then you have time to check the footage."

The other receptionist looked at him closely. "Well, pull it up."

"Seriously, Margaret?"

"I wanna see it!" she told him. Mr. Kingston sighed out loud, clicked a few times on his mouse, and his mouth dropped wide open.

"Okay, don't worry about the tardy slip. You're excused."

While that was good news, I looked at the clock in the office and saw it was already twenty minutes into class. I rushed up to the third floor and back to Ms. Ochoa's room. She asked for my tardy slip, but I told her it was excused.

"Fine, sit down and take your test."

I grabbed the test packet from her desk and started working. Most of the questions were summary questions about *The Crucible* like which character did what, where did the play take place, and why people were accused. But at the very end of the test, there was a short essay question about Giles Corey: *Why do you think Giles Corey never pleaded guilty or not guilty and was willing to be pressed to death? Would you have done the same? Answer in one handwritten page, minimum, one page and a half maximum.*

From what I remembered about the play, Mr. Corey's wife was also accused of witchcraft. I scribbled down a few sentences, basically saying Giles Corey wanted to stand in solidarity with his wife and if I had to support a friend, I'd do the same. It was a bunch of crap. At the Emerald Beach Shooting, I lied on the sand like a coward while someone shot my friends. I was the biggest coward on Rey Carlos Island. If anyone needed me to stand up for them, I wouldn't be able to. I was the weakest person I knew. When it came to bravery, I wasn't anywhere close to Giles Corey or the sailors on the USS Defiance.

"Time!" Ms. Ochoa said. "Pass your packets up to the front."

I hoped I did well. I never scored anything below a 90 in English, but I was worried. I didn't have a chance to look over my answers twice like always. The bell rang and everybody walked out to their last midterm. When I was at the door, Ms. Ochoa stopped me.

"Stay for a minute," she said.

"But I'll be late to my next class."

"Don't worry, I'll give you a pass. Are you okay?"

"What do you mean?" I asked.

"You've been quieter. I know you're always somewhat quiet, but you're pretty much silent now."

"Oh, I'm fine. Nothing's wrong."

"It's okay to have a hard time, Elysian. Don't think you have to hold your feelings inside. If you need to talk to someone, go ahead."

"No, I'm doing well," I said, even though my mind screamed: *tell her you have anxiety, moron!*

"Good luck on your next test," Ms. Ochoa said, handing me a hall pass. "See me if you need anything or someone to talk to."

I said goodbye to her and went down the semi-empty hallway to my history class. I walked inside Mr. Razo's classroom the second the bell rang. He told everyone to sit down and take out a pencil.

"I'm a nice teacher," he said, smiling. "So, this test is only two questions."

"Doesn't that mean each question will be worth fifty points?" asked Elizabeth Baines, the class idiot.

"Yes," Mr. Razo answered. "But they're easy. Take one sheet and pass the stack to the person behind you. Don't rush, don't fret, and don't talk."

When I got my sheet, I read over the questions three times each. Number one asked for the name of the archduke who was assassinated by Gavrilo Princip. The second question asked what happened as a result of the archduke's assassination. I knew the answers, but I was frozen for some reason. Mr. Razo had spent the last two weeks talking about this unit nonstop. *Why I couldn't think of the answers?* I pressed my pencil down on my sheet until it broke in half.

"Are you okay, Elysian?" Mr. Razo asked.

"Yes," I whispered, even though I was tired of lying all the time. I hadn't been okay in a long time. Then again, why should I tell the truth? My family said there was no such thing as anxiety.

They said I needed to toughen up, but I felt like I couldn't. It felt like anxiety was totally out of my control. Or maybe it *was* in my control and I just wasn't trying hard enough. It was probably my fault I had anxiety in the first place. Maybe if I tried toughening up, I could beat anxiety forever.

I thought about the morning lockdown and how I didn't know why we had one. I wondered about my parents and if they were okay. I thought about Emerald Beach having a second drive-by shooting. It was too much for me to handle. Before long, I was crying and my test was soaked.

"Elysian," Mr. Razo said, seated at his desk. "If you need a break, go ahead."

"I don't need a break," I said through my tears. "I need help."

"Come out with me to the hallway. Keep going, class! You're here until the last bell rings. No cheating! Santa Claus is watching!"

I walked out with Mr. Razo. We stood by a bulletin board with old school announcements that hadn't been replaced yet. Mr. Razo kneeled on the floor and looked up at me. He wore a tacky green suit and hadn't trimmed his facial hair. He looked like a comedian playing a teacher in an act.

"Now, now... I know you know who Princip shot. You're my best student."

"I can't remember," I said, mumbling. "I can't."

"The answer is on your shirt."

"What?" I looked down at my Franz Ferdinand shirt, one of my favorite bands, and felt like the biggest idiot on earth. "Sorry. I don't feel well. I haven't felt okay in months."

"Tell me about it," Mr. Razo said. "How do you feel?"

"Scared," I admitted. "Alone. Worried. Worthless."

"It sounds like you have anxiety."

"Huh?" I asked bewildered.

"Do you have anxiety?"

"I went to the ER for a bad panic attack a few weeks ago and the doctor diagnosed me. But my family says anxiety isn't real. So what's wrong with me?"

"Your family said anxiety isn't real? Are they stupid?"

I was shocked to hear Mr. Razo call someone stupid. He spoke with big words like Mom and Dad, but he always encouraged my classmates to keep trying, even Elizabeth.

"I... I don't know. What if they're right?"

"They're not. It's a real thing. I have anxiety, too. If I could turn it off, I would have done so years ago. Don't listen to them. I'm sorry to hear this, Elysian. You have a heavenly name, but you must feel like you're in hell all the time, huh?"

"What a ridiculous name," I said with a scoff. "My parents wanted me to have a heavenly name. Heaven isn't me."

"Stay after school for a minute and I'll give you some phone numbers," he said. "Don't worry about your test, I'll credit you the one hundred. I know you know the answers."

"Thanks."

"You're quite welcome. Let's go back inside."

Back in the classroom, I sat still in my seat. I breathed in and out slowly and imagined myself in my room, tucked in my bed, deep under the covers. I imagined Lalo texted me and said Gladys was home safe. The fantasies helped a lot and I was able to make it through the rest of class without another crying spell. When the bell rang, everyone ran out of the classroom except me. Mr. Razo asked me to have a seat by his desk. He got on his computer for a few minutes and printed out several sheets for me.

"I hope these resources can help you. The last one is important.

Be sure to call that number if you ever feel too sad."

The phone number was for the Rey Carlos Island Suicide Prevention Hotline, which I didn't even know existed. I wanted to tell Mr. Razo I wasn't suicidal since I was scared of everything and I would do anything possible to stay alive, but I didn't.

"Thanks," I told him. "Sorry about my crying."

"Nonsense. You don't have to apologize for your feelings. I'm not an asshole, I won't tell you have to feel a certain way. Oops, did I just curse?"

"You sure did."

"Detention for me then. Have a good afternoon, Elysian."

I left the classroom and headed to my locker to get my stuff. By then, the hallway was quiet, except for Lalo who whistled behind me as I loaded up my backpack.

"I've been waiting forever for you! What the heck were you doing? Pushing people all over the place?"

"I was pushing people to New Zealand!"

"Even the old ladies?"

"Especially the old ladies!"

"So you're on your way to Tiana's bakery?" he asked. "Can I come?"

"Sure, she didn't say only I could go."

"Awesome, then I'm going, too."

"Wanna invite Brandon?"

"We can, but he said he was going to the beach with his dad to collect cans. I'll text him."

We walked out of school together and made the first left on 5th Street. Pastry Pete's was at the very end of the street, tucked away between a dental office and a tutoring center. Tiana wasn't there when we went inside, but her dad, Mr. Serna, let us know she'd be on her way soon.

"Where'd she go?" Lalo asked.

"She ran to the grocery store with her mom for a minute. Can I get y'all started on something good while y'all wait? We have hot chocolate, fruit smoothies, ice cream, milkshakes, and over thirty kinds of pastries. What will it be?"

"I'll have a hot chocolate," I said.

"Mango smoothie, please," Lalo said. "And a chocolate chip cookie."

"Sure thing." We watched him whip up the hot chocolate and the mango smoothie. He popped Lalo's cookie in the microwave and served it on a small plate.

"Order 34!" Mr. Serna said, ringing a cowbell. We grabbed our orders and sat down at a little table in the center of the bakery. The hot chocolate was incredible. I don't know what Mr. Serna used, but it tasted so rich and creamy, I wanted a second one right away.

"Elysian, try this cookie," Lalo said, breaking me off a piece. "It's so damn good."

"It is," I said, biting into it. "We should come here more often."

Tiana and Mrs. Serna walked in, carrying huge brown bags filled to their tops with groceries. "Hey guys," Tiana said. They placed the bags down on the counter and Mr. Serna started putting everything away. "I'm glad you could come."

"Thanks," I said. "I loved the hot chocolate."

"It's my favorite. Hey, Eh-lee-shun, can I talk to you in the back?"

"Uhm, okay," I said, worrying about what she was going to tell me.

"Girl talk, I get it," Lalo said. "I'm gonna have another cookie."

I followed Tiana and she led me outside to the alley where the dumpsters were. There was a strong smell at first, but within a few seconds, it didn't bother me anymore.

"I have something to tell you," she said.

"Go ahead."

"But you have to promise you won't flip out."

"Why? Is it bad?"

"No," she said, twirling a curl on her hair. "Nate likes you."

"Oh my God."

"I told you not to flip out!"

"I'm not flipping out, I'm just not interested," I said. Shaky Boy Shakeface wasn't ugly, but from what I knew about him, we had nothing in common.

"Anyway, he wants to take you out on a date. Do you want to go?" I wanted to say *HELL NO AND IF YOU TRY TO MAKE ME, I'LL THROW YOU IN THE OCEAN!* Instead, I simply agreed in my lowest voice. "You will?! Oh my God! I have to text him right now! I can't wait to plan y'all's wedding ten years from now!"

"Huh? What?"

"You just said you'll go with him."

"I did?"

"Eh-lee-shun, don't act shy! I bet you like him back, don't you?"

She opened the back door to let me inside and rushed in, already on her phone, likely texting Nate to let him know I was available for his wooing. I wanted the floor to open up, swallow me whole, and spit me up somewhere else far away where I could start my life all over again.

"What the heck happened out there?" Lalo asked me. "Tiana blasted in here like she won a million bucks every day for life."

"She set me up with Nate."

"Nate?" Lalo asked, opening his eyes wider. "Are you kidding me?"

"I wish."

"Well, that blows harder a whale's blowhole. I knew we were lured in here for something. Tiana's sneaky."

After hanging out at Pastry Pete's for about an hour, Lalo and I told Tiana we were going home. Mrs. Serna offered to drive us, but we said we wanted to walk. As we walked down 5th Street, Lalo grunted. He'd take a step, grunt, take another step, and grunt again.

"Can you stop? You're making me nervous," I said.

"I'm upset."

"What's wrong?"

"Something is always wrong. Gladys is still gone. And I think it's super unfair of Tiana to set you up on a date with Nate. Date with Nate. Hey, that rhymes. Anyway, it was totally uncalled for and stupid."

"I can always cancel. I can say my religion doesn't let me date or something."

"Yeah, Elysian. Cancel as fast as you can."

When I got home, Aunt Sazón was making a huge pot of cheese ravioli for dinner and a butter cake for dessert. Uncle Pico sat on the couch, watching the news. He whined like Canelo every time they talked about politics. When a segment about a burglar came on, the reporter said he had escaped from custody and was caught by Madrazo Middle School. That explained the lockdown. Then the news cut away to a segment about Mark Pilsner. I didn't know what it was, but something about his face told me he didn't do it. Maybe it was only a gut feeling which meant nothing.

"The cops should shoot him already," Uncle Pico said.

"He hasn't had his trial yet," I said.

"Who cares? He did it."

"What if he didn't? Lots of people get arrested for crimes they didn't do. It's happened loads of times."

"Cops aren't idiots. If they arrest you, you're guilty."

"I didn't say cops are idiots, but they can make mistakes like everyone else."

"You always *have* to argue," Uncle Pico said, sighing. "I bet you'll grow up to be an attorney, but if you do, you won't have time for a husband or family. Look at your mother. She's a professor and you're stuck here being watched by your aunt. She should've picked you over her stupid job."

I wanted to punch him on his nose. I had no idea what Aunt Sazón saw in him. He seemed to get worse each time we interacted. Did she think a man being a completely uninformed, lazy asshole was extra sexy? Or, maybe she thought all men were the same and didn't bother to keep dating. If she had been in an arranged marriage or forced at gunpoint to marry Uncle Pico, I'd understand. But she willingly married an asshole.

"Why are you staring at me?" Uncle Pico asked. "Do you not have any manners? If I was your father, I'd spank you."

"If you were my father, I'd jump in front of a speeding bus."

For talking back, Aunt Sazón sent me to my room. She still gave me a plate of ravioli and a slice of butter cake, but she said I couldn't eat with everyone else. I didn't consider eating in my room by myself without hearing their dumb comments a punishment. While I ate, I heard my phone buzz. It was Brandon and he sent me a picture of the cans he and Mr. Meyer collected.

So many cans and we only got $10. What a waste.

Ten bucks is better than nothing.

This is crap. My dad needs to get another can finding buddy.

I finished eating and then flipped on my little TV. There weren't any shows that looked interesting, except for a documentary on the history of Galveston's immigration port. I watched a little bit and fell asleep before it was over. When I woke up in the middle of the night and checked my phone, I saw a text from a number I didn't recognize.

Hey, this is Nate. Can't wait to go out with you!

Chapter 14

On Saturday morning, I woke up with a soaked pillow.

"Ella!" I heard Aunt Sazón say from down the hall. "The A/C is broken. What's your friend Lalo's number?"

When I called Lalo and told him about the air conditioner, he said his dad was home, which was rare, and he'd tell him to come over.

"How much does he charge?" I asked.

"I dunno, I don't work with him."

"I'm not sure how much cash I have."

"Don't worry, Elysian," Lalo said. "He won't charge you anything."

"Cool. Hey, guess what? Nate texted me last night."

"Oh yeah? What did you tell him?"

"I haven't responded yet. I don't know what to say."

"Tell him to go to hell. And stay down there."

"But he didn't say anything bad."

"I don't care. My dad is on his way to your house."

When Mr. Richardson arrived, he rang the doorbell six times. He took a long breath and sniffed the air.

"Busted," he said, taking off his gray cap to scratch his head. "Where's the unit?"

"In the backyard."

"Take me to it."

I showed him where the unit was and Aunt Sazón came outside with us. Mr. Richardson pulled out some tools, took the entire unit apart, and within forty-five minutes, the unit was working again. Mr. Richardson rubbed sweat off his face with a little towel and tossed the tools back into his messy tool bag.

"You're fixed up," he said to Aunt Sazón and me. "No charge."

"Are you sure?" I asked.

"Hey, if you wanna pay, that's on you," he said. "I was letting you off the hook."

"Thank you, Mr. Lalo," Aunt Sazón said, shaking his hand.

"No ma'am, my name is Oliver Richardson, Lalo is my son... but you're very welcome. It was just a blown piece. You're lucky I had an extra one. Anything else?"

"That was it," I said. "Thanks."

"Welcome. By the way, Elysian, Lalo told me to tell you to cancel that date. Kid's been angry about it since yesterday."

"Really?" I asked, wishing Mr. Richardson hadn't opened his mouth.

"Cancel before he explodes and burns out. I don't have spare parts to fix him if he does."

The minute he left, Aunt Sazón turned to me. "First you disrespect your uncle, then you start dating boys behind my back? What has gotten into you, Ella?"

"My name is *Elysian*. And I'm not dating anyone."

"So Mr. Richardson lied?"

"There's a boy at school who wants to go on a date with me, but I'm not interested. I'm just gonna make up an excuse." But no matter what I said, Aunt Sazón wouldn't listen. She said boys were troublemakers who only wanted one thing, even though she never directly said what it was.

"If you think you're going out with a boy at your age, you're WRONG!"

"What is your problem? I already said I'm not going. I don't like him, he's not my type."

"So, now you have a type?! You're grounded!"

"What? Why?"

"You know why! Go to your room!"

I was telling the truth and I didn't understand why she didn't believe me. Whenever Ajo and Oregano had girlfriends, she never said anything to them about how dangerous girls were or how girls only wanted one thing. The whole situation made no sense. I wasn't sure who I could talk to about Aunt Sazón being unreasonable. After some thought, I texted Brandon.

Hey, can your dad call me?

He's taking a shower, but sure, why?

I have a question for him.

Okay. When he gets out, I'll let him know.

I waited twenty minutes, but just when I was about to text Brandon again, my phone rang.

"Elysian," Mr. Meyer said. "You have a question for me?"

"Yeah," I said, stepping into my closet and shutting the door behind me. "See, one of my... I guess, she's a friend... set me up on a date with this boy I don't like. Anyway, my aunt found out and she flipped, saying boys are trouble and I'm not allowed to go, even though I wasn't planning to anyway. What's the deal? I don't get why I'm in trouble."

"Classic double standard. Tell her she's stupid."

"I want to, but I can't."

"Elysian, I grew up in a community where women were expected to do absolutely nothing except get married and have kids. It sounds barbaric, but it's a widespread idea. Now she's right, a lot of boys only want one thing, but I'd trust you to go on a date. Or to skip one."

"What should I say then? Should I keep telling her I'm not going?"

"I told you, tell her she's stupid."

"Mr. Meyer..." I said with a sigh.

"I don't know, kid. It's up to you. If you go on the date, she'll freak and if you don't, she'll say you'll never meet anyone. Anything else?"

"No. Thanks, Mr. Meyer."

"No problem, Elysian. Take care of yourself."

"Wait," I said. "Do you remember any Torah verses or something? Something I can use as guidance for when people annoy me?"

"Uh," he said, clearing his throat. "Hmm. Well, there's something in the Talmud that says 'understand a man by his deeds.' I guess it means actions are louder than words. I used to be able to quote anything from the books, but now, I only know how to make an awesome BLT.'"

"Thanks again, Mr. Meyer. Bye for now."

I sat in my room for another hour and stared at the wall. Aunt Sazón was on the phone with Dad. I heard every word she said. She claimed I was head over heels and that no girl would claim she's not going on a date with a boy she likes. I walked out of my room and found Aunt Sazón yapping away on the couch with her feet up on the coffee table.

"I told you I'm not going on the stupid date!" I said. "Can I talk to my dad?"

"I'm speaking to your father," she said, putting her ear back to the phone. "Wait, what? You want to talk to her? Okay, here she is."

"Hi Dad," I said.

"Elysian, my heaven. You're not going on the date, are you?"

"No."

"I thought so. Your aunt is outrageous. I'll call you later, sweetie. Mom can't come to the phone right now, she's finishing her lecture notes. She says hi. Talk to you later!"

I handed Aunt Sazón her phone back. She looked up at me, shaking her head. "What did he say?"

"He believed me."

"I'm not your dad, I'm not biased,"

"Look, I said I wasn't going. Let's drop it."

"You need to drop your attitude. Boys don't like girls with attitudes."

"Aunt Sazón, I don't care what boys like."

"How can you say that? How will you ever get married?"

"I don't know. I'm fourteen, I don't care."

"But you need to have a husband someday."

"Whatever. If I get married, I'll get married. If I don't, then I don't."

By the afternoon, Aunt Sazón hadn't brought up the date anymore. I stayed in my room texting Brandon and Lalo and catching up on homework. Aunt Sazón was in the kitchen, making what smelled like grilled chicken and vegetables. When I finished my homework, my phone buzzed with a text from Nate.

So, when's our date?

I need to ask my aunt.

Okay, let me know when you find out.

I wasn't interested in him, but from what I saw, he seemed like a good enough guy. Within five minutes, my phone buzzed a second time. It was Tiana.

Hey! What's up? Nate is worried about you.

Why? Nothing happened.

Because he wants to go out with you, silly!

I know, I told him I had to ask my aunt.

Then ask! He's WAITING.

I didn't text back because if I did, it would have included curse words. It was my fault for going along with Tiana that day at Pastry Pete's. I should have never pretended to be her friend in the first place. Soon, I felt weird again. My breathing accelerated and my heart rate followed. For a minute, I thought about Nate. *What if he wasn't a good person? What if he only wanted benefits from me like help with biology homework from Dad?* I tried to stand up and walk around my room to calm down, but I fell on the floor as my thoughts raced more and more. *What if Nate was the best guy in the world? What if he was my future husband? What if this was the corniest love story in history?*

"Ella?" Aunt Sazón said, knocking on my door. "Are you okay?"

"Fine," I said as she opened my door and walked in. I was still shaking a little, but luckily she didn't notice.

"Why are you on the floor?"

"I was looking for something."

"Dinner is ready," she said before walking out. I remained stiff on the floor for a few more moments, but when I finally had the energy to stand, I regretted not staying on the floor, since Uncle Pico, Uncle Juke, Ajo, Oregano, and Canelo had just arrived.

"Elly!" Uncle Juke said when I reached the kitchen. "Glad you came out of your cave."

"Hi," I said, quickly walking to my spot at the dining table.

Uncle Pico sat across from me, reading the newspaper. He put the newspaper down the minute Aunt Sazón served him his hot plate of dinner. He stretched his arms up and sighed deeply.

"Another Gladys sighting," he said. "Yeah, whatever. Everyone knows the poor girl is dead and buried somewhere."

"We don't," I butted in. "Not yet."

"She's been gone for two months!" Uncle Pico said. "Stop lying to yourself. She's dead."

"Well, maybe she's not, Dad," Ajo said. "I read an article a while ago about some girls who were held hostage in some guy's house for ten years. They were still alive."

"Nobody would keep Glad Bag hostage," Uncle Pico said. "She wouldn't take orders from anyone."

"I think she ran away with a boy," Uncle Juke said. "Lots of women do."

"Maybe she got a new job," Oregano guessed. "One that's not legal."

"I think running away with a boy makes more sense," Aunt Sazón said as Canelo banged his fork on the table.

"*Or,* she was kidnapped..." I said. "Tons of people get kidnapped. Running away isn't like her. Even Lalo thinks so."

"What does he know? He's just a kid," Uncle Pico said.

"He's her brother!" I said.

"Ella!" Aunt Sazón said. "Don't yell at your uncle."

"Let her be, Katarina. She doesn't listen to authority," Uncle Pico answered.

"Ella, you need to be more respectful," Aunt Sazón told me.

I wanted to scream: *"You need to learn my name is not Ella, it's Elysian, not Eh-lee-shun, but Eh-lee-sea-un!"* But I stayed silent. My eyes shut and then my body shook.

Chapter 15

When I woke up, I was in my bedroom, tucked in my bed under several covers from the guest bedroom. Mom and Dad were on Aunt Sazón's phone. I heard Dad say, "Stop talking to me, put my girl on the phone."

With the tiny bit of energy I had, I sat up in bed. "Daddy?"

"There she is," he said, as the signal broke for a second, making his voice full of static. Aunt Sazón put her phone in front of me. Dad was on the camera, waving his hands around like he was trying to kill the largest mosquito in the world.

"My girlie!" he said. "What's wrong, sweetheart?"

"Huh?"

"Aunt Sazón told me you've been having anxiety attacks and had another one tonight. What's going on?"

"Oh," I said. I didn't want to tell him everything. I knew I could, but not with Aunt Sazón in the room. It was nice to hear he was concerned though.

"It's not so bad. I decided I'm going on the date with the boy I talked to you about. I'm probably just nervous about it—I don't like him in a romantic way. Yet."

"A boy!" Dad said. "That's my girl. Show him you're name brand, not store brand."

"Dad, you don't even know him."

"It doesn't matter, I already know he's not good enough for you."

Mom came on the camera next. She had her hair wrapped in a towel and her face was clean from makeup.

"Hi Mom, how was your day?" I asked.

"My day was exactly the same as many other days. I want to know how your day was. Did anything exciting happen? Did you learn something new?"

"No, my day was pretty usual, too."

"Anytime you need to talk, you know what to do. If I'm in class, I'll get back to you as soon as I can. Don't forget."

"I won't, Mom. Goodnight. Goodnight, Dad!"

"Goodnight, heavenly girl!" he said. "Sleep tight."

They signed off and Aunt Sazón's phone reverted to her home screen. She took a seat at the end of my bed, moved one of the covers on top of her knees and sighed. "I thought you were better now?"

"Nope."

"Have you tried breathing in and out?"

"Yep."

"Maybe you're not doing it right," she said with another sigh.

"Would you say that to someone who can't walk?" I asked, which I didn't mean to say out loud.

Aunt Sazón leaned back a little and squinted her eyes. "What does that have to do with this?"

"It's not as easy as you think. I don't have a magic switch in my head to turn off the anxiety. If I did, I would've turned it off a long time ago."

"You're in control of your mind," she said confidently. It's like she thought she was the biology professor and Dad was just some conspiracy nut on YouTube, claiming strawberry-flavored cough drops caused autism. "You can't convince me you're not. You own your mind. If you try harder, this anxiety thing will disappear."

"It won't."

"See? You don't even want to try," she said, rolling her eyes. "How can you expect to get better if you won't try?"

She would have been a pleasure to have around during the bubonic plague. *Oh, you're dying? Pus is coming out of your sores? You have a fever? You threw up a twelfth time? Why don't you just try to stop dying?*

"Goodnight, Aunt Sazón," I said, turning away from her.

She stood up, turned off my light, and stayed in my doorway for a minute. "Try to get some sleep," she said. "I read in a magazine that the brain works best when we get enough sleep." Then she shut the door behind her.

In the morning, I woke up to Uncle Juke screaming cuss words. I scrambled down the hallway and saw him pointing his middle fingers at the TV.

"What the hell are you doing?" I asked.

"These people," he said, pointing to the talk show. "They're saying men can control themselves around beautiful women!"

"Men *can* control themselves."

"BULL!" he said, pounding his fist on the couch. "If a beautiful woman walks in, I'm supposed to sit there and just leave her alone?"

"I don't know why you're upset," I said. I walked off to the kitchen before he kept speaking. There was half-eaten toast on the table and a near empty glass of orange juice, which I guessed was the waste from Uncle Juke's breakfast. Since Aunt Sazón hadn't left me anything for breakfast, I dug through the pantry for something to eat. I found strawberry toaster pastries, instant oatmeal, and some weird breakfast sausage in a can. I settled on a cracked strawberry toaster pastry. As I waited for it to pop up from the toaster, Uncle Juke continued his rampage in the living room. He yelled so loud, I thought the talk show hosts actually heard him. My pastry popped up, I grabbed it with a paper towel, took a bite, and immediately regretted it because it tasted terrible.

"Hey Ella!" he said, dragging out the last 'A' like Marlon Brando in *A Streetcar Named Desire*. "Glass of water, will ya?"

"Coming," I said. I poured his glass, handed it to him, and retreated to my room. I checked my phone and saw a notification for five new texts, all from Nate.

Hey Elysian

What's up

You doing anything today?

I'm at church, but it's boring

Want to meet up later?

I sat on my bed, clenching my teeth as I read his texts a second time. One part of me said "Just go on the damn date already," while another part said, "Don't be stupid, you're not even interested."

Sure. Where?

Within a minute, Nate called me. His voice wasn't shaky or cracked for once. He suggested ice cream at Jasper's and a walk around Emerald Beach.

"Hmm. It's a little hot today. How about the USS Defiance?"

"The big, boring ship?"

"Yeah, the big, boring ship."

"Okay, if that's what you wanna do. Can you meet up at one?"

"One is fine. See you later."

He hung up and then my phone dinged with a text from Tiana.

FINALLY! He's excited!

I didn't respond.

At noon, I took a shower and told Uncle Juke I was going out. He didn't ask too many questions because he was focused on a show about paranormal mysteries.

"You're going where?" he asked over the host's voice.

"USS Defiance."

"Have fun at Jasper's!"

Instead of going my usual way, I took a detour through Seashell Boulevard. It would take me longer to get to Emerald Beach, but I wasn't in a big hurry to get there. As I walked, my phone buzzed with texts from Tiana about Nate's favorite things. She said his favorite color was red, his favorite food was spaghetti with lots of parmesan cheese, his favorite book was *The Fault in Our Stars*, his favorite movie was *Life of Pi*, and his favorite hobby was building little models of airplanes.

Thanks, I texted back.

You guys are gonna have so much fun!

Nate was sitting at the main entrance of the USS Defiance when I arrived. He gulped down a cold bottle of water and stood up to salute me when I got close to him.

"What are you doing?" I asked.

"Saluting the madam."

"Let's go in," I answered as he trailed behind me. He paid for our tickets, but didn't want to sightsee right away. Instead, he wanted to share a bowl of ice cream at the deli.

"What flavor do you want?" he asked me.

"I don't care."

"Everyone has a favorite flavor."

"Not me. It depends on the day. Today, I'll take strawberry, I guess."

"Then we're getting strawberry," he said, winking his right eye.

While he ordered at the counter, I sat at a table with sticky residue. An older couple at the table across from me shared a root beer float. The husband was hunched over, trying to reach the tip of the straw, and his wife scooched the glass closer to him.

He took a sip and swallowed. "Thank you, dear," he said.

"Anything for you," she told him. I couldn't help but think about how lucky the husband was. If they had been Aunt Sazón and Uncle Pico, he would've said "Give me a root beer float, woman!" and she would've been her usual pushover self and given it to him.

Sometimes I wondered what Mom and Dad were like when they were abroad. When they were home, they showed affection. Outside of the house, they were reserved. They claimed professors had a reputation to keep, so they acted like professors on adrenaline injections whenever we went out. If they ordered something at a restaurant, they'd speak with extra exaggerated pronunciations. They always tipped the same amount as the bill, and if they needed something from the server, they would say "We apologize for the inconvenience, but may we acquire a side of ketchup for our French fries please?"

I wondered what they were like when they didn't feel the need to keep up their reputation, when no one who knew them was watching, when they could kick back and be their true selves. My true self was nowhere to be found. I was living one day at a time, one anxiety attack to the next, trying to piece myself together, but the pieces weren't matching up.

"I got sprinkles," Nate said as he sat down with our big bowl of ice cream. "They had crushed cookie pieces, too, but I didn't know if you wanted them."

"Sprinkles are good," I said, trying a spoonful of the ice cream, even though it was too heavy and sweet.

"Everything okay?" Nate asked.

"Yeah, everything is fine."

I ate a few more spoonfuls of ice cream, but Nate ate most of it. When he finished, we walked around the USS Defiance. Unlike me, Nate wasn't interested. He'd read parts of the information on the walls, yawn, and say things like "The sailors on this boat must've been bored to death."

"They were at war, they probably peed their pants from fear every day," I said.

"Didn't they know what they signed up for?"

"Some of them were drafted, they had to go."

"You're lucky you're a girl. You'll never be drafted. You get to stay home and be safe. I gotta sign up for the draft when I turn eighteen like every guy."

"I don't think it's fair. Why shouldn't I have to sign up? What if all the boys on American soil die? Then what would happen?"

"How would all the boys die?" he asked, laughing.

"It can happen," I said, even though the idea sounded impossible when I thought about it. "Let's go to the medical area," I said, trying to change the subject because I felt my heart sprinting. "It's my favorite section."

"That's all the way across the ship."

"So? We don't have to go in order." He groaned, but came along behind me.

"I wonder if there are any ghosts in here," Nate said as we entered the medical area. He was shaking a little, but since it was freezing, I didn't know if it was his genuine shaking or not.

"I doubt it."

"You're a ghost denier?"

"Well, I don't know. If they are real, they're not trying to scare us. At least, I don't think they are."

"Why wouldn't they?" he asked, leaning over the wall in the dental office to see better as the *"ouch, my gosh darn it, dagnabbit aching tooth!"* recording played in the background.

"Think about it," I said. "If you were a ghost, you'd be minding your own business, doing ghost stuff. Then someone sees you and they freak out. It wouldn't be your fault."

"When you put it like that, they don't sound scary."

In the surgery room, Nate looked at everything, but not for long. He kept looking at his phone. I couldn't tell if he was texting Tiana or playing a game. Eventually, I pulled out my phone and texted Brandon.

I'm out with Nate.

Yeah? You guys having milkSHAKES?

Shut up, Brandon.

I put my phone down when Nate turned around. He rubbed his eyes and yawned. "I'm fed up with this place. Let's go somewhere else."

We left the USS Defiance and walked along the west pier to a souvenir shop called Surfin' Samantha's Souvenirs. Loads of tourists were inside buying batches of worthless crap they'd forget about once they got home. Nate picked up a turtle keychain with the words "Rey Carlos Island" on its belly.

"This is kinda cute," he said. "I'll get this for Tiana. Are you gonna buy anything?"

"Nope, I live here. I don't need a reminder."

"I moved here two years ago from Corpus Christi. My mom got a job at the aquarium. She's a marine biologist."

"Corpus has an aquarium, too."

"They do, but not like the one here. This one is much bigger and does more research. Have you always lived here?"

"I was born in Ecuador. My parents moved here when I was two, so pretty much, yeah. Do you like it here? I think it's kinda boring."

"I mean, it's all right. It's just like Corpus, but I don't have friends here except you and Tiana. And Brandon and Lalo too, I guess. He scares me though."

"Lalo?" I asked, laughing in his face. "He's not scary. He's a sweetie."

"Is he? Every time I'm around him, he gets, like... uhm, I don't know... tense? Maybe that's not the right word. It's like he's a hungry tiger and I'm a sandwich."

"I don't know what you're talking about," I said, picking up a necklace. It was one of those cheap ones with a thin chain and a name. When I looked at the name, my heart dropped.

Gladys.

I thought about buying it and giving it to Lalo, so he could hold on to it until Gladys was found, even though my anxiety said I shouldn't because Gladys was dead and was never coming home.

"I'm gonna buy this," I declared, holding up the necklace so Nate could read the name.

"That's not your name."

"My name is never on anything. I'm getting this for Lalo. It can remind him of his sister."

"Wait, are you talking about the missing lady?"

"Yes Nate. It's been on the news since the beach shooting."

"Gladys Richardson is Lalo's sister?" Nate asked. "Dang. Well, no wonder he's always moody. I didn't know his sister was missing."

"He has the right to be moody for as long as he wants."

"She probably ran away with a boy," Nate said. "Or maybe she was pregnant and didn't want people to know."

At the register, we waited behind a line of tourists. Nate touched everything by us which irritated me all the way down my spine. He grabbed magnets and rearranged them, put pencils in other cups, picked up stickers and placed them elsewhere. I wanted to grab him by his ears and scream, *STOP DESTROYING THE STORE, YOU IDIOT* but I managed to stay quiet.

"Next!" the sleepy cashier said. Nate put his keychain on the counter and reached his hand out to me.

"I got the necklace," he said.

"No, let me get it," I insisted. "It's for Lalo."

"So? It's only three bucks."

"Kid, there's a line, let the girl pay for her own necklace or scram," the cashier said. Nate paid for his keychain and then I paid for the necklace. The cashier slid the necklace into a small paper bag and stamped the surface with the words SURFIN' SAMANTHA'S. We left the shop close to five.

"I'm gonna run home," I told Nate. "I need to eat dinner with my uncles, aunt, and my stupid cousins. I might as well sit on the beach and eat with the crabs."

"Yeah, I should get going. So, are we official now? Can I put it on Snapchat?"

"No, we're not official."

"What?! But this was a date, wasn't it? I paid for everything."

"That doesn't make it a date. We're friends."

"How many more dates do I need to pay for before we are official?" he asked.

I wanted to lift him up by his ears and throw him off the pier. "You can't be serious. *Please* tell me you're not serious."

"Isn't that how it goes?"

"You can't buy a person's feelings, Nate."

"Whatever. I won't post anything on Snapchat then. Can I text you later?"

"Yeah, sure. I'll be home."

I walked away from Nate as fast as I could. The date, if it was one, wasn't horrible, but it wasn't great either. While I walked, I thought about Lalo. He told me to cancel the date before it even happened. I didn't listen because I was stupid. I texted Lalo to see if he was home.

You at your house?

Yeah, he said *Mourning.*

Mourning what?

Your day. You killed it by going out with Nate.

Damn. Cold one I texted.

If you come over, ring the doorbell twice so I know it's you.

The sun seemed heavier as I reached my neighborhood. By the time I got to Lalo's, I was out of breath. I needed water, stat.

"Well, well, well," Lalo said when he opened the door. "It's Mrs. Shakerson."

"Just give me some water, Lalo. I feel like I'm a witch burning at the stake."

"There's cold bottles in the fridge," he said. I followed him inside to the kitchen where he had been folding kitchen towels. I opened the refrigerator, grabbed an ice cold bottle, and guzzled the water down.

"How was your engagement party?" he asked.

"We just went to the USS Defiance and Surfin' Samantha's."

"I bet he's posting it on Snapchat right now."

"He is not. I told him not to."

"Good."

"Here, I got this for you," I said, handing him the paper bag. He took it, opened it, and pulled the necklace out. The thing was so cheap, the chain broke in half the second he placed it on the kitchen table.

"Oh," he said, reading the name. "It's nice. Thank you."

"I thought you'd like it."

"I do. I'll save it for her. She loves to fix broken things. That's why she married Octavio."

"Sorry it broke. I can get you another one."

"No, don't worry about it. Do you want a snack or something?"

"No, I'm fine. I need to get home. I'll text you later tonight."

"Bye Elysian. Or should I say Mrs. Nate Whatever-His-Last-Name-Is-Because-I-Forgot."

"Whatever, *Eduardo*."

"Hey!" he said, holding a wrinkled towel in his hands. "Nobody calls me Eduardo!"

"I don't get why your parents named you that, if they were just going to call you Lalo all the time anyway."

"They didn't," he said. "Gladys called me Lalo first and they went with it."

"It's better than Eduardo. That sounds like something people say when they get hurt."

"What?" he said, almost dropping the last towel on the floor. "How on earth does it sound like that?"

"Think about it. Eh-du-ar-dooooo... say it in slow motion."

"Why? My name is Lalo."

"Shut up."

"I'll talk to you later," he said. "I gotta finish these towels. There are more in the dryer."

I left Lalo's and got home before anyone else. It was extra

quiet for once. Aunt Sazón texted and said she'd be there by eight at the latest, since she was out with Ajo, Oregano, and Canelo. I was relieved that Uncle Pico and Uncle Juke must've had other things to do.

I got hungry around 6:30, but there wasn't much to eat. I thought about ordering a pizza and chicken wings. I counted the cash in my wallet. Nine bucks. Nowhere near enough for wings. Then I remembered Dad's habit of hiding money around the house.

I went to the master bedroom, peeked and poked around the bathroom, under the bed, the dresser, and the nightstand, but I didn't find anything. I decided to check one last spot. Dad had a huge elephant paperweight, ornate and heavy enough to hold down a real elephant. Dad claimed the trunk came off and it was a good idea to hide valuables in the opening. Maybe he wasn't kidding. I went inside the home office, saw stacks of papers about topics I didn't understand, dusty books, the off-center globe, and I found the elephant on one of the bookcases. I tried getting it down, but it was way too heavy. I hopped on a stool, tugged at the trunk, and it slipped off. There wasn't any money, just a tiny piece of paper with one of Dad's theories about the genetics of webbed feet. His handwriting was worse than a hurricane, so I couldn't make out what it said. I stuffed it back into the elephant and settled on having only pizza for dinner.

I called Forno's, a parlor on Sandstone Boulevard. They had a five-dollar special for a small cheese pizza, but they wouldn't deliver unless I spent $15. I told the lady on the phone I'd pick my order up. After I hung up, I realized I needed a Plan B.

"Yo," Brandon said when I called him. "What up?"

"Is your dad home?"

"Until eight."

"Can you guys pick up a pizza for me? I have the money, I'll pay you back."

"Yeah, no problem," he said. "Daaaaad! Elysian needs a pizza!"

"We all do!" I heard Mr. Meyer say in the background.

While I waited, I watched a documentary about the Zodiac Killer. It was interesting, but it scared me after a few minutes because the Zodiac had never been caught. The murders had happened a long time ago, but my mind tried to convince me there was a 100-year-old out there, still killing people. There was a sketch on the screen of the Zodiac from one of his incidents. He wore a black, square shaped hood and sunglasses over the hood. I wondered why he never got caught and why he went on a killing spree. He seemed smart from what the documentary said. It was sad he invested his entire intelligence, as Mom would say, in something negative instead of something positive.

"To this day, we still don't know if the Zodiac Killer was more than one person," the narrator on the documentary said. "We may never know. For now, let's get into a few of the theories..."

Aunt Sazón walked in with Canelo behind her, carrying grocery bags in her arms and asked me to get the rest from the car.

"I ordered myself a pizza," I said. "Brandon and Mr. Meyer went to get it for me."

"Pizza?" she said, rolling her eyes. "That's not dinner."

"I'm hungry. I don't know how to cook yet."

"When I was your age, I cooked everything. Your mom needs to teach you. How will you ever get married if you can't cook? Do you think your husband will cook for you?"

"If I marry a chef, sure."

"Oh, you think you're special? Let me tell you something,

Elly... men don't like women who talk back."

"Boo-hoo. I'm gonna go get the groceries."

It was dark outside, but the two street lights by my house helped. Mr. Meyer and Brandon pulled up. The aroma of melted cheese, oregano, garlic, and buttered crust was extremely pleasant.

"Pizza! Pizza, pizza, pizza!" Mr. Meyer shouted. "We got pizza for Elysian!"

"Smells amazing," Brandon said. "We got one for ourselves, too."

"You guys can come inside, my hands are full," I said. "I have your money, Mr. Meyer."

"Don't worry about it. This pizza is from me, the pizza wizard."

They exited the car and headed to the front door. Aunt Sazón let them inside, but not without a few looks. I trailed behind them with the heavy grocery bags. When I was able to put them down at last, my arms shook from the weight.

"Are you two staying for dinner?" Aunt Sazón asked, which was code for *get out and don't come back.*

"Nope," Mr. Meyer said. "We got a pizza for ourselves in the car. I gotta go to work in an hour anyway."

"What do you do again, Mr. Meyer?" she asked, only wanting to know so she could talk trash about him.

"I'm a bouncer at Isle of Darkness. I tell people they can come in, I tell losers they can't, and I beat the crap out of people who start fights. Long hours, hard nights, but hey, someone's gotta do the job."

"A bouncer," Aunt Sazón said. "What a unique career."

"It's better than being at a job I hate."

After they left, Aunt Sazón showed me how to make rice. She

said I had to measure the water, place the rice in the hot pot with butter and garlic, and then add the water in and sprinkle salt on top.

Canelo wouldn't stop screaming. He ran through my house, pretending he was an undercover spy, because undercover spies have to be as loud as they possibly can.

"Are you paying attention, Elysian?" Aunt Sazón asked. "You have to know how to make rice. It's a basic staple food."

"Can you tell Canelo to quiet down? He's distracting me."

"He's just expressing himself. He loves to play pretend. You never know, maybe he will be a spy someday."

I couldn't understand the parallel idea. Canelo got to run around, fantasizing about his future, and I was stuck in the kitchen with Aunt Sazón learning how to make rice.

"If the spoon stands up straight in the center of the pot, it means the rice is ready," Aunt Sazón said. "You did well for a first timer. A year from now, you'll be making rice better than your mom."

"What's wrong with my mom's rice?"

"She barely knows how to make it. She's busy with work. She might be super smart in academics, but she can't make your dad a decent pot of rice."

"My dad doesn't care about rice," I said. "Intelligent men like intelligent women."

Chapter 16

Three months had passed since the Emerald Beach Shooting and since Gladys went missing. The load of cop cars hadn't gotten smaller. The news often reminded everyone on the island to be safe. Mark Pilsner was still in jail, waiting on his court date. At school, we were getting ready for Thanksgiving break, which meant loads of tests, quizzes, and projects. I caught strep throat in the middle of everything. I didn't want to miss school, but I had to.

I stayed in bed and Aunt Sazón stayed home with me. She'd bring me a bowl of homemade chicken soup every three hours and lots of water, even though it hurt to drink anything. I texted Lalo and Brandon throughout the day. They were supposed to be paying attention at school, but they were texting me back within seconds.

Dude, Nate is freaked out that you're not here Brandon texted.

Well, he's gonna have to deal with it. I'm super sick.

Perfect time to come kiss him, so he'll get sick and be off your back.

Brandon, don't you have a quiz?

I'm done. It was easy.

He texted me a picture of himself with a bored face. Lalo was behind him, making the peace sign with his fingers. His black hair went well with his blue eyes.

Lalo says hey. He misses you. Get well soon.

I'll try.

After lunch, Aunt Sazón sat with me in my room. She told me boring stories about my grandparents. They owned a little restaurant close to downtown Guayaquil until Grandpa Rafael had a stroke and couldn't work anymore. Mom almost never talked about my grandparents. I knew the basics about them like what they looked like, when they were born, when they died and what they died of. I wasn't overly curious about them. They died years before I was born. Even if they were alive, I doubted they'd be involved in my life. If they didn't want to be involved with Mom, why would they be involved with me?

"Your grandparents were wonderful," Aunt Sazón said at the end of her last boring story. Maybe they were wonderful to Aunt Sazón and Juke, but they were horrible to Mom.

"I'm gonna take a nap," I said with strain in my voice. "I'm sleepy."

"Go ahead," Aunt Sazón said. "A sick girl needs rest."

She got up and walked out. I wasn't sleepy—I just wanted her to leave. I scrolled through my phone for the latest news on Gladys. There were more articles on sightings, but nothing with any leads or clues. Octavio had been interviewed by *Houston Chronicle* a few days earlier. He talked about how caring Gladys was and how easy it was for her to help others. He thought she was lured by someone who appeared to need a helping hand and she went along thinking she was doing the right thing, but ended up making a terrible mistake. There were many theories about Gladys. I couldn't wait to ask her what happened. I couldn't wait for Lalo to see her again.

At five o'clock, Lalo texted me, needing help with math homework. I tried my best to help him but I got stuck, too.

This is hard, Elysian, I wanna drop out.
You can't drop out, you're only fourteen.
Man, I'll fix A/Cs with my dad. How are you feeling?
Sick!
Get better ASAP, I need math help.
Whatever. You're a riot.
Better than Nate.

I had another bowl of soup for dinner. I felt lucky to be sick and sit out from dinner with my family, since they were being loud as ever. I heard them talk about what happened to Gladys, my parents being gone, and what they planned to buy for Christmas. Aunt Sazón mentioned I'd be alone for Thanksgiving and she wanted Ajo, Oregano, and Canelo to be extra nice to me.

"Ma, she's *so* weird," Oregano said. "She's always mad. She's never been normal. Girls are supposed to be happy."

"Yeah Mom," Ajo agreed. "What's her problem?"

"She's too independent," Uncle Pico said. "Her parents let her hang out with boys, they let her go out without supervising her, it's horrible. If she were my daughter, she wouldn't be the way she is now."

I couldn't pinpoint what was terrible about me. Was I not allowed to feel a certain way just because they said so? They got offended whenever I didn't bow down to their backwards ideas. Who was the real problem then? Me or them?

"She's young," Aunt Sazón said. "She has time to grow up and change."

Change into what? A toaster? I thought to myself.

"She needs to meet a good boy," Uncle Juke said, chewing louder than tacky wallpaper. "If she met a nice boy, she would change to make him happy."

Nope. Wrong again.

In the middle of their enlightening conversation, I fell asleep. I dreamed Mom and Dad were home. Mom was wearing her best red blazer and Dad was in his signature navy suit. Even if they were gone for semesters at a time, it was nice to have them as my parents. They were the smartest people I knew. But I wished they weren't, so they wouldn't be invited to teach at other universities all the time. When I woke up, I checked my phone. It was only 9:15. I texted Lalo and asked him if he figured out his math homework.

Hell no, I'm more lost than an Amish dude who just got a cellphone.

It can't be that hard.

Elysian, I wanna drop out.

Don't, you're smart.

Yeah, yeah.

As I lied in bed, Nate texted me. He wanted to know if I was awake but I didn't answer. He texted me again at 10:30 with a picture of himself. His lips were pursed up, like he was blowing me a kiss or imitating a duck. I gagged at the sight.

Check this out, I texted Lalo and sent him the picture. Within a minute, he texted me back.

Dang. He's ugly.

He's not ugly, he's just making a weird face.

Sticking up for him, huh?

Yes, Lalo. I'm in love. I'm gonna drink poison like in Romeo and Juliet.

Everybody died and it's a romance story? Barf. Barfeo and Barfliet.

I laughed out loud, even though it hurt my throat.

I'm going to bed, I'm pretty sick.

Kiss Nate!

Shut up or I'll kiss you to make you sick and shut up.

Kiss me? Why would you kiss me?

I dunno, Lalo, I'm just talking.

Oh. Well, if you want to, we can. I don't care.

I wasn't sure how to respond. Was he kidding? Was he trying to say something else? I reread his text over and over. He texted me again before I could think of an answer.

Omg please don't freak out, I'm so sorry. You can kiss me if you want or not if you don't want to. Please don't kill me.

I didn't know what else to say. *What?* I texted.

You don't have to kiss me, Elysian.

No, I mean, it's fine. I can.

You would?

Sure. You're not Nate.

Yeah man, screw Nate. Shaking shaker boy.

Goodnight Lalo, I'll text you tomorrow.

Okay, sleep well.

I tightened the covers around my body, shivering from chills thanks to my fever. It was almost midnight by the time I fell asleep.

The next morning, I dragged myself to the kitchen where I found Uncle Pico sprawled on the couch, eating plantain chips straight out of the bag. He took a big sigh and said good morning. I don't know what it was, but his face looked more punchable than ever.

"What's wrong?" he asked. Even his voice was punchable.

"Nothing, I'm tired," I lied.

"Your aunt made pancakes, but they're not good."

"Why not?"

"She put too much flour. They're thicker than a pretty lady's legs. Eat them if you want. I threw mine out."

"Where is she anyway?"

"She's working again. Her time off is over. You're stuck with me."

"I'm gonna eat, I guess," I said. It was easier to talk than the day before.

"Use lots of syrup to get those pancakes down, so you don't choke. I don't know CPR."

"I won't choke." I walked to the kitchen, looked around, and found a plate with aluminum foil on top. I peeled it off and there were the thicker-than-cement pancakes. I doused them in syrup, which only made them soggy. I threw them out and settled on eating yogurt for breakfast instead.

"Hey Ella!" Uncle Pico said from the living room. "Come here!"

I went over and found him pointing at the TV. There was a report about Mark Pilsner. A little girl had been exploring an abandoned building in the southern tip of Rey Carlos Island unsupervised and found the gun used in the Emerald Beach shooting. "I saw something on the floor and then I noticed it was a gun! Pow pow!" she said. There were fingerprints on the gun, but they didn't match Mark Pilsner.

"I knew it," I said.

"Can't believe this," Uncle Pico said. "I thought they had the son of a bitch."

"I'm so glad to be out of jail," Mark Pilsner said on the TV screen. "I didn't shoot those people. I don't know who did, but it sure as hell wasn't me. The only thing I use to shoot is my camera."

I was happy to see him walk free. But then I thought about the real problem: whoever committed the shooting was still out there.

"These cops are back to square one, huh?" Uncle Pico said.

"They can't find a hat in a hat store, dumb morons."

"I hope they find the person," I said, swallowing the mucus stuck in my throat. "At least an innocent man isn't in jail anymore."

Later that day, Uncle Pico went to the store. Uncle Juke came in his place and immediately flipped on the TV to the naughty channels. He told me he hoped I didn't mind.

"You have no idea how much I mind," I said. "Can't you watch something else?"

"It's no big deal," he said, motioning his hands to the TV. "Ain't that bad."

"I'm going to my room," I said, dashing off. I sat there for a minute before deciding to text Lalo, but he actually texted me first.

Nate asked me about you. He said you didn't text him back.

Tell him I don't feel well.

I did. But he wants you to text him back anyway.

Fine. I will.

Hey, so, are we gonna make out? I need to know. I need to fold towels again later.

Today? No! I'm sick!

Oh yeah.

I hopped on my computer and checked out the assignments I was missing. I missed a quiz in history and a test in science. My other homework assignments were worksheets and reading chapters in my textbooks.

I started working until Dad called me about thirty minutes into my homework session. "My girl," he said. "Your aunt said you caught strep. How are you feeling?"

"Still sick, but better than yesterday."

"When are you going back to school?"

"Thursday. I wanted to go back tomorrow, but Doctor Bal-livián signed my note for Thursday, because I'm contagious."

"Stay home, get the rest you need," Dad said. "Mom says hi. She's giving a lecture right now. I was listening in for a little bit and I was blown away. Every time she talks, it's amazing. How on earth did she get so brilliant when her family is so... well, you know."

"I do."

"Get well soon. I'll tell Mom to call you when she's done for today. We'll be back in about five weeks. Are you excited?"

"Very."

"You don't sound like it."

I wanted to say *I'm not super excited because you and Mom will just leave again,* but I didn't. "I mean... yeah, I am," I said finally.

"I'll talk to you later, Elysian. My heavenly daughter."

"Don't say that, it sounds like I'm dead."

"But you are heavenly. Mom and I wanted a girl. When you were born, Heaven came straight down to us."

"Thanks Dad," I said. "I'll talk to you later." I hung up, touched by what he said, but also frustrated. *If I was heavenly, how come he and Mom always left me?*

By Wednesday morning, I felt much better. I was happy to find myself home alone. Aunt Sazón texted me that there was oatmeal, fruit, and turkey bacon in the refrigerator for whenever I wanted to eat breakfast. I turned on the TV to the morning news and grabbed my breakfast. I sat in front of the TV, savoring each bit of my food. The news talked about the weather first and then they had another report on Mark Pilsner being let free. They were interviewing people on the street, asking them what they thought. Almost everyone said they couldn't believe the police department was letting him get away with attempted murder.

"And now an update on Gladys Richardson," the reporter said. "A sighting has been reported in Dallas at a local restaurant called Terelli's. Police are investigating if the sighting was indeed Richardson."

They showed a photo of the person who was supposed to be Gladys, but it looked absolutely nothing like her. At this point, someone could see a potato walking down the street and claim it was her.

Watching the news, I texted to Lalo. *Another Gladys sighting.*

Not her. My parents already talked to the cops.

It didn't look like her.

The lady looked 60. Gladys is 22. What the hell is wrong with people?

No idea. I'm feeling better, finally.

Good. You need to text Nate and tell him to get lost. He keeps asking about you.

I realized I hadn't texted Nate back yet and scrolled through my phone to get his number. Before I could send a message, Tiana's name popped up on my screen.

Hey girl! Are you okay? I know you've been sick.

Yeah, I'm fine.

Nate wants a SECOND date!!!!

Yay?

Yes, YAY!!!!!!! So, when's date number 2?

I don't know.

C'mon! He's HEAD OVER HEELS for you.

Great.

Couldn't she tell I wasn't interested? Why was she acting like the matchmaker of Rey Carlos Island?

I'll think about it, I texted.

Think about what? Nate ADORES you!

I didn't text Tiana back and since I was dead focused on what to say to her later, I forgot to text Nate. Around four in the afternoon, he texted me.

Elysian? Are you better?

I'm better. I'll be at school tomorrow.

Good. I miss you.

I had strep, so be careful.

Haha. I will.

I spent the rest of the evening watching a documentary about the USS Defiance. It came on at seven, right when Aunt Sazón served dinner, but I wanted to watch it, so I asked her if I could take dinner in my room instead.

"It's better to eat dinner as a family," she said.

"I'm still contagious though."

"Oh. Well, yes, you can eat in your room. Be careful not to spill anything on the floor."

"I'll be careful."

Aunt Sazón, Uncle Pico, Uncle Juke, Ajo, Oregano, and Canelo were loud as hell as usual. I turned the volume up on my TV to drown them out. The documentary opened up with the plans of the USS Defiance. The navy wanted a strong warship, one strong enough to take anything. When the USS Defiance was completed, Galveston wanted it to be docked there, but Rey Carlos Island turned out to be better because its part of the ocean was tamer. The documentary showed pictures of the USS Defiance when it was brand new and ready to take on naval battles. It looked way different, even bigger than what I had seen in person. The documentary cut away to photos of the sailors, captains, cooks, and other crew members of the USS Defiance during World War II. The narrator said while 557 men died on the ship, 530 were lost at sea through various attacks. I couldn't imagine how their families must have felt. It couldn't have been great news for the families to find out a loved one had died, but at least they had closure.

The whole thing got me thinking about Gladys. *What if her abductor murdered her and threw her in the ocean? Lalo would never have closure like those families. She went missing in August and it was already November. She was dead. Gladys was in the ocean, lost at sea and her body would never be found. Then another thought popped in my head telling me she might still be alive, but not doing well. Where the hell was she? Why did this person take her? What really happened that day on Emerald Beach?*

"Ella?" Aunt Sazón said, knocking on my door. "Did you eat? Do you need anything else? I made chopped mandarins and whipped cream for dessert. Would you like a bowl?"

"No, I'm fine."

"Are you sure?"

"Yeah."

"Okay. I'll leave a bowl in the refrigerator if you change your mind."

I wrapped the covers around myself until I stopped panicking and fell asleep.

Chapter 17

When I went back to school, Nate found me the minute I walked in and handed me a fake rose with the tag still on. I shoved it into my backpack, and when I checked on it in math class, it had broken in three pieces.

"Cheapskate," Lalo said. "Couldn't bother to give you a real rose."

"A real rose would just die."

"What can you do with a fake one?"

"Dude, I don't know," I said, sighing. "I'm sick of him."

"Why don't you tell him off?"

"I don't want Tiana coming after me. I've seen *Mean Girls*."

"She won't do anything, she needs us to get to Brandon. Go on a second date and tell him how you really feel."

"Are you serious? I'll puke."

"Then puke. Nobody finds that attractive."

After I returned home, Aunt Sazón was finishing dinner and was in the middle of washing the dishes. "Hi," she said. "How was school?"

"Fine. Same stuff."

"Do you have homework?"

"Of course."

I grabbed a bag of peanut butter sandwich crackers from the

pantry and locked myself in my room to get my homework done. I did math first, followed by the rest. By the time I finished, it was six. I grabbed my phone and group texted Lalo and Brandon.

About to set up the second date, what should I say?

Brandon Meyer: *Hell if I know.*

Lalo Richardson: *Meet up somewhere public.*

Emerald Beach? It was the most public area I could think of, even if I hated going there.

Lalo Richardson: *Perfect.*

Brandon Meyer: *Or get shakin' at the club.*

We can't go clubbing, we're too young.

Brandon Meyer: *Young people go clubbing. My dad lets them in if they pay him enough.*

Lalo Richardson: *He can get in trouble for that.*

Brandon Meyer: *They don't pay him enough to care.*

I took a deep breath and thought of what I'd say to Nate. How did I end up with a boy after me anyway? For my entire life, I had heard *Boys don't like girls like you* and suddenly, here was a boy who was interested.

Hey Nate, I texted.

He immediately texted back. *Hi! So, where do you want to go? I'm free tomorrow.*

The beach? After school?

Yeah! We can have ice cream at Jasper's, he texted.

Okay.

Awesome. I'll see you tomorrow, cutie.

Puke 1, Elysian 0.

"Ella!" Aunt Sazón said from the living room. "Your cousins are here! Dinnertime!"

Puke 2, Elysian 0.

I sat at the dinner table across from Uncle Pico with Uncle

Juke on my left. Ajo, Oregano, and Canelo sat in the center and Aunt Sazón was hanging off from the last chair at the edge of the table. She made grilled chicken with rosemary sauce, mashed potatoes, and chopped vegetables. The food was good, but the company was terrible.

"So I hear you know how to make rice now?" Uncle Pico asked. "That's good. A girl like you should know a proper skill like that."

"Oh yeah," I said. "Every time a girl learns how to make rice, the angels in Heaven sing and God cries tears of joy."

"That's the spirit," he said. "Soon you'll be making a meal like this one."

"It'll be my fondest dream come true," I said as Aunt Sazón looked at me with a scrunched nose.

Uncle Juke cleared his throat. "You know, men like a woman who can cook."

"Your theory is wrong," I blurted out. "There's a boy at school who already likes me."

Everyone at the table dropped their silverware and sat in silence. They stared at me with eyes like still moons. Was it really that unbelievable?

"Who?" Uncle Pico asked, breaking the awkward silence.

"His name is Nate. He's kind of tall, I guess. He has brown hair and brown eyes. I think he's Hispanic, but I don't actually know."

"You're way too young for this, Elly," Aunt Sazón said. "Best thing to do is not get involved. When you're sixteen, maybe."

"I hate to break it to you, Aunt Sazón, but you're not my mom." I didn't know what my parents thought about dating because we never talked about it. We never had time to talk about anything.

"Be careful," Ajo said. "Sometimes guys lie about who they

are. Don't always believe what they tell you."

"Yeah," Oregano agreed. "Just be careful. Be safe."

"MORE CHICKEN!" Canelo screamed.

The rest of dinner was quiet. When I finished eating, I washed my plate and utensils and went to my room where I laid in bed, goofing off on my phone. I looked up stupid topics like "do penguins have knees?" and "how many toes does an elephant have?"

Around bedtime, I got a text from Brandon.

Yo.

Hey Brandon.

Man, I don't know what it is, but I feel like you shouldn't go on that date.

Why?

I dunno. Just a guess.

You and Lalo can be around checking up on me.

Yeah? That's okay?

Of course, it's okay. Get bouncer tips from your dad.

Easy. Cover your face and head. Punch in the stomach.

Night, Brandon.

Hey, I'm watching a show about Ted Bundy. I ain't sleeping tonight. This guy was EVIL. The name Ted sounds so, I dunno, not evil. Goodnight.

I turned off my light and laid in bed. I heard Uncle Pico and Aunt Sazón rambling in the living room about me. Uncle Pico swore there was no way any boy would like me because I didn't act like a real girl. Aunt Sazón told him there was still time for me to learn how to be a real girl, but since I was stubborn, she wasn't sure I'd learn in time. I put on my slippers and rushed to the living room.

"Ella!" Aunt Sazón said. "What's going on? Did you have a

nightmare?"

"No, *you're* the nightmare."

"Me? I'm here watching you, cooking for you, doing whatever you need while your parents are away... and I'm a nightmare?"

"Apologize to your aunt, Elly," Uncle Pico said, his lips clasped together like a clothespin as Aunt Sazón stood by him.

"You've got to be kidding me. First of all, I *am* a real girl. Just because I don't do whatever the hell you think girls should do, doesn't mean I'm any less of one. If I were a boy, you two would treat me so differently. It's not my fault I'm not a boy. I'm a real girl and I don't give a shiiiiiiit about what you think!"

I ran back to my room, slammed the door, and went into my closet. I dropped to my knees and cried so hard, I thought my head would pop off my neck. *Were they right about me? Was I not a real girl? Was there something incredibly wrong with me and I didn't deserve to be a real girl?*

"Open this door, Ella! Now!" Aunt Sazón said, knocking. "Open up!"

I stayed in my closet, drying my tears with an old University of Houston sweater I got a few years before. It was almost eleven. I knew Brandon was busy watching his murder documentaries instead of sleeping. I texted Lalo, but I was pretty sure he was asleep.

Hey.

Hey Elysian, what's up?

Oh. You're still awake?

Nope. I'm a burglar. I robbed Lalo at gunpoint and now I'm folding his towels.

Shut up, Lalo.

What's up?

Can you call me?

Within a minute, his name and picture popped up on my screen. I picked up as Aunt Sazón banged on my door.

"What's going on?"

"Oh, I'm okay," I said, with my voice was breaking. Before long, I started crying again.

"Elysian?" Lalo said. "Are you crying? What's wrong?"

"I was trying to go to bed and I heard my aunt and my uncle saying I'm not a real girl and there's no way any boy could like me. Am I really that bad? Why can't I be normal? Listen to me crying about this and Gladys is missing. I'm selfish."

"You're not being selfish. You're having a hard time. And that's okay. My hard time isn't worse than yours. It's not a contest."

"Thanks."

"And you are a real girl. You're the realest girl I know."

"How do you know?" I asked.

"I mean, I don't know what makes a girl real or not. But I don't see how you aren't one."

"They said it's because I don't know how to cook, I talk back, and other stuff I don't remember right now," I said, sniffling. "Then they said they couldn't believe a boy could like me if I'm not a real girl."

"Hah! They're wrong. There is a boy who likes you a lot."

"Yeah, but it's Nate."

"Nate's a boy," he said. "And I'm a boy, too."

"What does that have to do with anything?"

"Nothing, never mind. Hey, try to get some sleep. Don't listen to them."

"It's hard not to, they're here all the time until my parents get back..." I heard a big slam followed by a thud. I peeked out of my closet door and saw my bedroom door on the floor as Aunt

Sazón and Uncle Pico barged inside.

"I gotta go," I told Lalo.

"No problem, I'll see you tomorrow."

I hung up the phone and slowly walked out to my room. Aunt Sazón pointed at me and commanded me to look at her. "You will apologize to me right now! The way you're acting is not okay."

"So it's okay for you and Uncle Pico to talk about how it's impossible for any boy to like me? It's okay for you to say I'm not a real girl? I'm never apologizing to you. I did nothing wrong. You should apologize to me."

"That does it," Uncle Pico said. "Time for you to learn respect!"

His slap left a hand imprint on my cheek. I cried out and he slapped me a second time, before pushing me down to the floor. My whole bedroom felt like it was spinning. I took a deep breath and exhaled a sob. "Don't ever come to my house again!" I yelled.

"You don't own this house, Ella. Your parents do," Aunt Sazón said.

"My parents will be home soon. Get out, Pico!"

"You needed that, Ella," Uncle Pico said. "It's long overdue."

He walked out and Aunt Sazón followed him. I wanted to call my parents, but I figured they were asleep since it was past one in the morning in Buenos Aires, so I emailed them instead. It was the first thing they checked every morning.

They must have still been up, because Dad called me five minutes after I sent my email. "Elysian? Are you okay?"

"I think so," I said. "Maybe. It was scary."

"Put him on the phone."

"Why?"

"*Elysian Lecaro*, put... him... on... the phone."

I went to the living room where I found Aunt Sazón and Uncle Pico watching a late-night talk show. I handed the phone to him and he took it from me gently. For once, he didn't have his typical stern expression. In fact, he looked worried.

I have no idea what Dad said to Uncle Pico, but the next morning, as I sleepily got ready for school, Aunt Sazón told me Uncle Pico wouldn't be coming over anymore.

"Not even for dinner?" I asked.

"No, he'll eat at our house."

"Good."

When I got to school, I waited for Lalo and Brandon in the courtyard. Brandon showed up first, his eyes a deep pink.

"No sleep?" I asked him.

"Man, there was a good documentary after the Ted Bundy one about Hinterkaifeck Farm."

"You're obsessed with that case."

"I wanna know who did it!"

"Brandon, it was almost a hundred years ago. Whoever did it is long dead now. You can't bring a dead body to court."

"Yeah, you can. There was a pope who was dug up and put on trial. I think he was found guilty too. Look it up."

"No thanks. Don't want to gross myself out."

Lalo got to school right before the first bell rang. He said his dad brought him to school and drove extra slowly. "He got a speeding ticket a week ago, so now he's being super careful. It's ridiculous. He was going slower than a snail. Anyway, I got your text, Elysian. What did you wanna tell us?"

"Oh," I said, wondering if I should or not. They were my best friends, but they were also boys. I felt like there were things I couldn't talk to them about because they wouldn't understand. I never talked to them about how uncomfortable bras could be or how cute boys are when they're polite. Would they understand why Uncle Pico put his hands on me? Would they understand what it felt like not being considered a real girl? "My uncle slapped me and shoved me to the floor last night."

"Son of a bitch!" Brandon said, lightly punching his left palm with his right fist. "Where's that motherfucker at? I'll pound his nuts off."

"Your uncle hurt you?" Lalo asked. "Why? What happened?"

"He broke my door down, so my aunt came in and told me to apologize. I said no, and within like two seconds, I was on the floor."

"What a cowardly dipshit," Brandon said as the bell rang and everybody scattered in different directions. "We'll talk later. Tell me all the details."

"Me too," Lalo said.

At lunch, Tiana shoved her way to our table with Nate. He gave me another dollar store rose and dark chocolate truffles. I bit into one of the bitter truffles and forced myself to swallow.

"You guys are so cute together!" Tiana said. "I can't wait for y'all's wedding!"

Puke 3, Elysian o.

"I'm not gonna pass math this year," Lalo said. "I'll do summer school."

"Math isn't too bad," Brandon said. "Better than geology."

"Geology is way easier. You only have to remember the names of the rocks," Lalo said.

"And when they form, where they form, why they form, all that load of crap," Brandon said. "It's ridiculous. I'm never gonna need to know this stuff when I'm out in the real world."

"If you're a detective, you can figure out which rocks can kill someone," I said. "You could tell by the dust left behind at the crime scene."

"You'd make such a great detective," Tiana said, her eyes nearly popping out of their sockets. "You are soooo smart."

"Street smart," Brandon said. "Detectives gotta be street smart to figure shit out."

After school, I walked with Nate to Emerald Beach. I texted Brandon and Lalo to let them know we were going. We didn't get ice cream at Jasper's because of the long line, so we bought snow cones from a cart close to the marina.

"Let's sit on that bench," Nate said, pointing a finger in its direction. "There's shade."

"It's not hot though," I said, feeling uneasy. I didn't know why. There was no reason for me to feel uncomfortable. We took a seat and ate our snow cones which tasted horrible. No wonder there hadn't been a line. Nate was done with his first. He swung his empty cup into a trash can a distance away from us and it landed right inside.

"Good shot," I said, nibbling away at my trash cone.

"Thanks. I wanna try out for basketball in high school," he said. "I talked to Tiana last night. She told me sometimes you freak out about stuff. Is that true?"

"What?"

"She said you get scared and start breathing really hard."

"Oh," I said, placing the rest of my half-eaten cone underneath the bench.

"Is that a disease?" he asked. My first reaction was anger, but then I thought maybe he just didn't know and was curious.

"I have anxiety. It's not contagious. There are ways to handle it, but no cure, sadly. So yeah, sometimes I do freak out."

"Hmmm... you can't stop it?"

"If I could, I would've stopped it a long time ago."

"That's interesting," he said, rubbing sweat off his nose with his shirt. "I'm not sure I can handle your anxiety when it happens."

"Well, that's fantastic because you don't need to," I said, standing up.

"Wait, where are you going?" he asked, his eyes wide open. "I thought this was a date?"

"*Was* is the key word. I'm done."

"Hold on, give me a chance," he said, rushing after me. I tried walking faster, but he caught up and tugged at my shirt.

"Nate, I don't know what Tiana's been telling you, but I'm not interested. I was gonna tell you nicely, but now you're pissing me off."

"Is this a freak out? What's wrong?"

"No, this isn't one of my freak outs! Leave me alone. I'm going home."

"You're being weird. I didn't mean anything bad. I said I couldn't handle your freak outs, but maybe I can if I try hard enough."

"Nate, let me go," I said, pulling my shirttail away from his grip, but he wouldn't leave. He followed me down the boardwalk, all the way to the deck leading to the USS Defiance. I wished it was still in function and a sailor could blow a cannonball at him.

"Stop," Nate said. "And listen to me."

"For what?" I said, speeding up my pace.

He didn't say anything else. Instead, he grabbed me by my shirttail again and forced his tongue into my mouth. I pushed him away, but he was attempting a second kiss when I heard "Let go of her right now!" from behind me. I turned around and saw Lalo running towards us. Nate mumbled something to himself before taking off in the opposite direction as I stood there, stunned.

"Did he hurt you?" Lalo asked, waving his clenched fists around. "I'll smack him with my towels if he did!"

"You were spying?" I said.

"Spying? No, I was supervising."

"You mean, you were here the whole time?"

"Duh, Elysian. You texted me and Brandon about this. I was gonna come with him, but he had to go to urgent care. I just got here a minute ago. Sorry I'm late, I didn't mean to be."

"What's wrong with Brandon?"

"It's not him, it's his dad," Lalo said. "He has a fever. He's had one for days."

Chapter 18

Mr. Meyer's fever turned out to be a bad case of stomach flu. He spent six days in the hospital. I visited him with Brandon on the fourth day. He had fluids hooked up and a monitor that took his blood pressure every fifteen minutes.

"This damn thing's at it again!" he screamed at the monitor. "My pressure ain't any higher or lower than fifteen minutes ago, you piece of shit!"

"Dad, stop screaming, it's just a machine," Brandon said. "How are you feeling?"

"I threw up nine times yesterday, but today I've only thrown up five times," Mr. Meyer said, squirming in his bed. "So I guess I'm getting better."

"Did you eat something rotten?" I asked him. "What did the doctor say?"

"She said I gotta lose weight, exercise more, quit smoking, watch what I eat, shit nobody wants to hear," Mr. Meyer said, shaking his fist at the monitor. "She's not too thin herself either."

"She's right, Dad," Brandon said. "At least stop smoking."

"I spent eighteen years with people telling me what to do, Brandon. You're not about to do the same."

"Dad, chill out! I just want you to live longer! Damn!"

"What are you talking about? I have a stomach flu, not bubonic plague."

"I get it, Dad, you wanna do whatever you want. You can keep being a bouncer, you can keep eating all the non-kosher foods, but what about me? I want you to get older. I don't want you dying young, because you couldn't put the cigarettes down." I looked at Brandon in shock. It was the most sympathetic I had ever seen him.

Mr. Meyer grunted and cleared his throat. "Fine."

"Hey, at least you can eat pork, right?" Brandon said. "Eat all the ham sandwiches."

"Hell yeah, I'll eat all the ham sandwiches," Mr. Meyer shot back. "All the bacon, all the salami, all the bologna. *ALL OF IT.*"

"Cool," Brandon said. "No more smoking. Hell, while you're at it, no more drinking either. Got it, Dad?"

"Yeah boss, I got it. There's twenty bucks in my wallet, get yourself and Elysian something to eat."

Brandon and I hung out in the hospital cafeteria, sharing a small order of French fries while waiting for Lalo to join us. We . They were extra salty, so I only ate a few. Brandon's eyes were swollen, his cheeks drooped, and his black hair was all over the place.

"Damn, man," he said. "I'm tired. When I got shot in the ass, I didn't even stay in the hospital this long. What the hell?"

"Have you talked to your mom?"

"Yeah, she told me to make sure Dad doesn't flip out at the nurses. He hasn't, so far. He needs all the chill pills they got in here."

"When do you think she'll come visit?"

"Hell if I know. She's four hours away."

Lalo showed up at last with a fresh scratch on his left cheek and a yogurt cup and pretzels.

"What happened?" I asked when he sat down.

"What are you talking about?"

"You have a big scratch on your cheek. Are you okay?"

"Oh," he said. "Uh. Yeah."

"You didn't get in a gang fight, did you?" Brandon said, laughing. "My man Lalo. Fighting gang members with towels."

"I'm fine," Lalo said, darting his eyes around the cafeteria. "A hundred percent."

Before we left the hospital, we visited Mr. Meyer in his room one last time. He constantly yelled at the blood pressure monitor and then swore to us that he was okay.

"Dad, quit it," Brandon said. "Enough is enough."

"When I'm out of here, I'll be as strong as a bull again."

"You don't need to be," Brandon said. "Take a break. You need one."

"I'm okay," Mr. Meyer repeated. "Don't worry."

When we left the hospital, we walked to Brandon's house. There were dishes piled in the sink, mail stacked on the table, and dry groceries in their original bags that hadn't been put away. The kitchen floor had stains from old spills. I took a paper towel from its holder by the kitchen sink, wet it, and wiped what I could, but the residue was too caked.

"Leave that stain alone, Elysian, I'll get it. It's been such a mess these last few days," Brandon said. "And I'm by myself."

"Maybe you can stay with me," Lalo said. "I'll ask my parents, I'm sure they'd be fine with it. You can help me fold towels."

"Yeah," Brandon said. "I'm sick of this alone life."

"Isn't there another job your dad can do?" I asked. "Like anything else?"

"Man, I guess. Bouncer is probably all he can do unless he goes to night school, which he won't do unless they serve ham sandwiches."

For a minute, I felt lucky. If my parents wanted another job, they had a better shot since they had the education. They would definitely be professors until the days of their funerals, but in the worst case scenario, I knew they would have lots of job options if they needed to change careers. Mr. Meyer would most likely have to be a bouncer for a long time, at least until he wasn't able to beat up people anymore.

"I texted my parents, they said you can stay with us," Lalo said to Brandon. "Pack up your stuff and walk home with me."

"All right, thanks," Brandon said, heading to his room. Lalo and I waited for him in the kitchen, munching on carrot sticks we found in the refrigerator since they were the only things that hadn't spoiled yet.

"My grandparents are coming to town for Thanksgiving," Lalo said. "I know my dad will be home, but I'm not sure about my mom. She works holidays. It sucks."

"Emergencies don't take days off."

"Yeah, I know, but it still sucks. Everybody else has their parents home on Thanksgiving and Christmas. How come I can't? It's not fair."

"I hear you. I miss my parents a lot, too."

"I know you do. By the way, have you heard from Nate?"

"No, not since that awful second date."

"Good. I don't think you will hear from him again. You may see him at school, but he won't bother you anymore."

"How do you know?"

"I just know."

When Brandon was ready to go, we walked to Lalo's house. It

was a little after five and the sun was setting, so we picked up the pace and got to Lalo's house quickly. To our surprise, Mrs. Richardson was there, eating dinner in the living room along with Mr. Richardson.

"Brandon," Mr. Richardson said, still wearing his signature gray cap. "Come sit with us, we have lots of food left."

"Oh, thanks," Brandon said. "I'm not too hungry though."

"When you are, there's plenty," Mrs. Richardson said. The bags under her eyes were so heavy, they looked like trash bags.

"Don't you want some food, Elysian?" Mr. Richardson asked me. "Text or call your aunt first and find out if she doesn't want you spoiling your dinner."

I texted Aunt Sazón to ask her if she had already cooked.

Canelo wanted chicken noodle soup, I'm in the middle of making it. Give me an hour or hour and a half until it's done.

I can eat dinner here at Lalo's, his mom made arroz con pollo and salad.

Do that. I'll pick you up later.

Mrs. Richardson served me a plate, and when I was done, I licked my fork several times. She served Brandon one too and he ate everything in a few minutes.

"Mrs. R, this food is freaking awesome," Brandon said. "My dad can't cook anything."

"Thank you, Brandon," Mrs. Richardson said. "My pleasure."

While I waited for Aunt Sazón to pick me up, I watched TV with Lalo and Brandon in Lalo's bedroom. We skimmed channels and settled on watching an old Garfield cartoon.

"A talking cat?" Brandon said. "What the hell is this?"

"It's Garfield," I said. "My mom loves this comic."

"This is weird," Brandon said. "He's just a huge, sarcastic cat."

"He's basically you if you were a cat," Lalo said. "Minus the murder mystery facts."

When Aunt Sazón texted to tell me she was outside, I said bye to Brandon and Lalo and Mr. and Mrs. Richardson before heading out to her car. She smelled of seasonings and humidity.

"How was your day?" she asked when I was in the car. "Did you visit Mr. Meyer?"

"I did. He's doing okay. He needs to stay for observation for two more days."

"If he ate healthier food and exercised, he'd be in better shape," Aunt Sazón said. She always had a solution to everything since she was the most brilliant person on earth.

"Maybe. He's stubborn though."

"Oh, yes," she said, nodding her head. "He's something else. I wonder if he's still in the Jewish cult thing."

"I wouldn't say it's a cult," I said. "Cults have a supreme, human leader. From what he's told me, he grew up in a strict, religious community."

"We don't know for sure that he's not wanting to rejoin," Aunt Sazón said.

"He's not going to. He loves ham too much."

Aunt Sazón pulled into my driveway. We went inside and she made me a cup of hot chocolate, even though it wasn't cold outside anymore. I took a sip and added a sugar packet to dull the bitter taste of the Ecuadorian hot chocolate. I hated it, but Mom and Dad loved it so much, they'd bought bulk packages from eBay.

"How's the boy you were talking about?" Aunt Sazón asked. "Does he like you?"

"I dunno. I don't care if he does or not. I'm not interested."

"Oh, I wasn't interested in Uncle Pico either. He asked me out on a date over ten times before I said yes. He wouldn't take no for an answer. Isn't that sweet? That doesn't happen nowadays anymore."

I wanted to say *That's because refusing to take no for an answer is super creepy and messed up,* but I kept my mouth shut.

"So what's the issue with this boy? Is he weird?" she asked.

"He kissed me without asking first."

"On the cheek?"

"Oh no, on my mouth."

"Hmph. He needs to ask next time."

"He won't be kissing me a second time."

I was disappointed Nate was my first kiss. It was unwanted, gross, and the most unromantic thing ever. I didn't think about kissing boys a lot. The few times I did, I didn't picture anyone like Nate. I always thought it'd be awkward, but cute like in teen romance movies. I never thought it would be so horrible, I would want to jump off the boardwalk and go live with dolphins like a sea version of *Tarzan.* I thought about what it would be like to kiss Brandon. He'd kiss me and then tell me how many body parts Ed Gein kept in his dresser drawer. Then I thought about kissing Lalo. We still hadn't, even though we had talked about it. I couldn't picture him rushing to kiss me or him drooling everywhere. If he did drool, I knew he'd have a clean towel.

"When's dinner?" I asked Aunt Sazón. "I'm hungry again."

"I left your bowl at my house," she said. "Stay right here and let me run over there."

The minute she walked out the door, I texted Lalo.

You alone?

Yeah. Brandon passed out already. He was reading a Reddit about the Sodder Children, I think.

Are you still up for a kiss sometime?

What? Right now?

No, not right now. I don't want tacos de lengua before I go to bed.

Haha. You're funny. Whenever you want tacos de lengua, aquí estoy, mi preciosa.

Shut up, Lalo.

You shut up, go push people.

Okay. So tomorrow?

Yeah. Tomorrow.

Aunt Sazón came back with a bowl of chicken noodle soup and a pitcher of guava juice. It was nice to eat without snide comments every minute for once. Aunt Sazón mostly scrolled her phone, probably texting Uncle Pico or Uncle Juke. She looked up at me a couple times, but didn't say much besides "how's the soup?" or "more juice?"

After I ate, I got ready for bed. I was able to work Dad's old radio, too. A song called "Walk on the Wild Side" came on. From the lyrics I could make out through the static, it was a song about being yourself, even if it meant being completely different than everyone else. I don't remember when I first felt different, but I think it was when I didn't get my neighborhood nickname. I was only Elysian, the girl named after the heavenly Elysian Fields. The Elysian Fields were a paradise in Greek mythology, a place everyone wanted to go to. But here I was, alone with only my hellish mind.

Chapter 19

The next day, I arrived at school early. I hung around the courtyard, listening to the water flow from the fountain in the center and the wind swirl through the walkways. Texas was hot on most days, but since it was almost Thanksgiving, the weather wasn't scorching anymore. I texted Lalo and asked him where he was. He was supposed to come to school early for math tutorials, but he wasn't anywhere in sight.

Woke up late, Dad is driving me.

C'mon Lalo, you're gonna flunk math if you don't take it seriously.

Hey, when is math gonna kiss me? Am I right???

What the hell are you talking about??? You can't make out with algebra, you freak.

Make out? I thought we were only kissing? Dang, Elysian. Now you got me excited.

Whatever Lalo, I'll see you later.

When it was close to the first bell, I saw Tiana with a tight, pissed off expression. "What the *heck*, Eh-lee-shun?" she said, approaching me. "Are you kidding me? What's your problem?"

"What are you talking about?"

"Don't pretend," she said with her face in mine. "You know exactly what happened!"

"So because Nate kissed me even though I told him not to,

that makes me the bad guy? Get a grip on yourself."

"What? He didn't tell me about that," she said. "Lalo beat him up!"

"Whaaaaat? Lalo? No way," I said, laughing until my face warmed. "Nate must've gotten him mixed up with someone else."

"No, I was there. It was right outside Nate's house. Lalo gave him a black eye."

"Wow, what a fighter." I said. *Lalo Richardson, lightweight champion. Ruuuuuuumble Riiiiiiiichardson!* "I had no idea. I'm not into Nate, sorry. But I had nothing to do with Lalo pounding him a black eye."

"Yeah, I guess," she said, sitting next to me. "I'm sorry about Nate kissing you. He told me you guys kissed and then you flipped out on him."

"I didn't want to kiss him. He forced me to."

"But I'm confused," she said, bouncing her backpack on her knee. "If you didn't wanna go out with him, why did you?"

"I wanted to be nice. How is he anyway? You know... aside from the black eye?"

"He's okay. He doesn't wanna hang out with us anymore though."

"Good."

"I'm sorry again," Tiana said, her backpack still on a horsey ride. "You know, I think you're pretty cool. You're interesting. Even your name is unique."

"Thanks. It's pronounced *Eh-lee-sea-un* by the way."

"So cool," she said. "*Eh-lee-shun!*"

"Good Lord," I said, but she didn't hear me.

After school, Lalo and I walked to Emerald Beach. We didn't stop by Jasper's, but we got corn in a cup from a cart stand called

Mr. Elotero. The corn was way too spicy for me, so I let Lalo have mine.

"Aw man," he said. "You didn't like it?"

"It tastes like fire."

"Eh, it does," he agreed, tossing both cups into the trash can. "I don't wanna taste like a volcano when I kiss you. Where do you want to kiss anyway?"

"Hmm, how about the USS Defiance?"

"Oh. I don't know if I have enough money to get in."

"It's Tuesday, students are free today. Let's go."

We got in line behind some high school boys going on and on about how hot Samantha Vanderbilt was and how Mrs. Kaufmann's rack was big enough to hang clothes on.

"What is with these guys?" Lalo said. "Who checks out their teacher?"

"Lots of people do."

"I can't look at my teacher like that. They're like a billion years old. It'd be like checking out my grandma."

"Lalo, our teachers aren't dinosaur fossils."

"Well, they're much older. Old enough to make me feel weird."

Once we were inside, we browsed around the main areas first before going to the deeper ends of the ship. Lalo climbed up on some stairs and stuck his face in a sailor cutout.

"Look at me! Sailor Richardson!"

"You could never be a sailor, you're a bad swimmer."

"What? I'm the greatest swimmer ever. I could outswim a shark."

"A shark would eat you in one bite."

"Shut up," he said, coming down from the corny cutout. We walked to the boiler room, which had grinding sound effects followed by a man's voice saying, "Get back to work!" Lalo read all of the info plaques, even the longer ones. Every so often, he'd say, "Wow, that's pretty cool." After the boiler room, we went to the medical area, which was its usual Arctic wind temperature. We laughed out loud at the recording in the dental office.

"I swear it gets funnier every time," I said. "You know what would be hilarious? If that's really how the sailors on this ship talked."

"No way. My dad used to be in the Marines. The way he talks is more colorful than a pack of crayons."

We reached the end of the tour faster than I expected. I looked at my phone and saw it was already past five. The USS Defiance closed at six, so we had a little time to keep looking around if we wanted. I took a seat on one of the chapel pews. I expected Lalo to sit by me, but he was busy looking at something in the corner of the room.

"Hey, look," he said, pointing to a ladder. "I wonder where those steps go."

"I don't think we can go up there. Plus, that's a narrow ladder."

"It's not that bad," he said, already a quarter up the ladder. "I'll go up there myself and tell you what I find."

"Okay, I'll be down here." My mind said he'd lose his balance and topple down the ladder and break his neck. Another part of my mind said he'd be fine. Grazed, I remembered. He was never shot. He was grazed. He was okay then. He'd be okay now.

"Whooooooooa," I heard him say. "Elysian, you gotta come up here!"

"You can't make me."

"You gotta! Get on the ladder!"

"Lalo, I told you I'm not going up there."

"It's safe. If it wasn't, I wouldn't tell you to come up."

I sighed, stood up, and started my way up. All of the ladders on the USS Defiance were narrower than Uncle Pico's views on women, but this particular ladder was even narrower than that. I held on tightly to the sides. When I reached the top, Lalo stuck out his hand and helped me stand. It was an observation deck, cramped, hot, and a little damp, but the view made up for everything. We could see all of Rey Carlos Island. The sun was going down. The waves of the ocean were a deeper shade of blue, calmly beating against the glittery sand. This was how I pictured my first kiss.

"Okay, nobody's up here but us," he said. "You ready?"

"I am."

"Are you sure? I'm not gonna kiss you if you're not ready."

"I'm ready," I said, squeezing his forearm. "You got me up those nightmare steps, let's do this."

"All right. But, this is my first kiss. I YouTubed how to do it, I subscribed to a couple channels, I read Reddit threads, and went on Instagram. If this kiss sucks, I'm super sorry."

"You YouTubed how to kiss?" I asked, laughing. "*And* you went on Reddit? Isn't that for murder mysteries?"

"Reddit? No, there are threads about everything. Anyway, let's do this before someone finds us, if that's okay."

"If I change my mind, is it okay if I tell you to stop?"

"Hell yeah. It's your mouth, not mine."

He inched closer to me, looked into my eyes, brushed away the hair from my face, took a deep breath, and slowly put his tongue in my mouth. At first, it was almost as bad as the kiss with Nate, but then it got better. There wasn't as much as drool. The kiss felt *right*. He even asked "is this still good or should I stop?" a few times.

"Thanks," I said when we were done. "We should head home."

"Yeah," he said with a nod. "I'm not getting locked in here. There are probably sailor ghosts."

"Sailor ghosts?"

"A bunch of people died in here, there have to be ghosts walking around. Oh man, what if someone died on this deck?"

"Well if someone died on this deck, we just made out on their spot. Let's get out of here before we get cursed."

"Right behind you. You go down first."

I made my way down the ladder and praised God when I reached the chapel below. Lalo came down behind me and then we left the USS Defiance through the giftshop doors.

"So, what did you think?" Lalo asked as we headed home. "Were those YouTube videos and Reddit threads any good? They better have been."

"I liked it a lot."

"Cool... do you wanna kiss again sometime?"

"Uhm," I said, feeling myself blush. I wanted to kiss him again and again, but the darkness of the night was coming on too soon. "Yeah."

"Me too. Not today though. We got a quiz in freakin' math tomorrow."

"Oh, I've been meaning to tell you," I said when we got to the intersection. "Thanks for beating up Nate."

"Dang. I told him and Tiana not to say anything!"

"You don't have to beat up people for me, Lalo."

"I do when they're mean to you."

"Yeah? You're going to beat up my uncles and my aunt?"

"Elysian," he said, rubbing the back of his head with his left palm. "I know this is gonna sound about as corny as... uhm... the corn cups we threw away, but I would do anything for you. I'm glad you stayed on the sand before the shooting started. If you had been by me, I would have taken the bullet for you though."

"Are you serious?"

"Of course. If you haven't figured it out already, I like you. I like you a lot."

"You've got to be joking."

"No, I'm not. Why would I joke about liking you?"

"Because I have anxiety attacks. I freak out. I worry about *everything*. Why would you like me?"

"Your attacks don't last very long. There are twenty-four hours in the day and if you have one that lasts an hour, that's still just a tiny part of the day. It doesn't bother me. It's a small part of who you are and that's okay."

"Thanks," I said.

When we were down the street from our houses, I glanced at my phone and saw Aunt Sazón had texted me three times.

Where are you?

Answer your phone, young lady.

If you are not home by 6:30, you're in BIG trouble.

It was 6:15. I had fifteen minutes left. We were outside his house, standing on the empty driveway. He took out his keys from his back pocket and jingled them.

"Get home before your aunt flips out. And tell her I only like real girls."

I watched him rush inside and wave to me before I bolted home. When I got in, Aunt Sazón was in the kitchen with her arms crossed over her chest. "Where have you been?"

"It's 6:30. I made it home on time."

"You did. But where were you?"

"Why does it matter?" I asked, turning my back to her.

"Because you're fourteen and I'm watching you while your parents are away."

"I was at the USS Defiance."

"Alone?"

"No, I went with Lalo for a school project."

"School project?" she asked with a long sigh. "Oregano was there, too."

Crap, I thought. *I bet that weasel was spying on us.*

"Did you have fun?"

"Yeah, I love the USS Defiance," I said, sitting down at the table. "I had a lot of fun."

"I'm sure you did. I can't believe you're lying to me about dating that boy!"

"Says who? Oregano?"

"He saw you and Lalo looking around the ship, being *extra* playful. You're fourteen, Ella. Boys only want one thing, especially boys like Lalo."

"If boys are so bad, why did you marry one?" I asked.

She took a big gulp. "Lalo's no good for you."

"Oh wow!" I said, laughing. "You mean you have dating advice for me? I can't tell you how much I'd *love* to marry a lazy ass like Uncle Pico who bosses me around all the time. The angels in Heaven would sing."

Aunt Sazón walked away from the kitchen and into the guest bathroom, where I heard her talking to my parents about my so-called attitude. She said I was becoming a brat and needed proper discipline before it was too late to change me. Then she told them about how Oregano had seen me and Lalo having way too much fun and how someone needed to talk to me about boys before I got myself pregnant. While she ranted endlessly, I texted Lalo.

My aunt flipped out. Oregano saw us at USS Defiance.

Nooooooooo, damn it.

He didn't see us kiss.

Yessssssss.

Can we kiss again soon?

Elysian, you can kiss me whenever you want.

Are you sure you like me?

I do.

You like me with all my flaws?

Yeah, man. I like you. A lot.

I drowned out Aunt Sazón's voice by thinking of other things. I thought about Gladys coming home. I thought about Mom and Dad being home. I thought about Brandon and Mr. Meyer's relationship changing into something closer. Then Lalo popped in my head. I couldn't believe he had a crush on me. My mind said, *There's no way in hell he likes you. He's scamming you.*

But my mind also said, *You've known him forever. He doesn't scam people. He's Lalo, for God's sake. The worst he's done is forget to fold the towels.*

For the first time in years, I felt wanted.

Chapter 20

The next morning, Aunt Sazón woke me up extra early because my parents were on the phone. I took her phone in my left hand, hit the speaker button, and let out a drawn-out yawn. "Morning, Mom. Morning, Dad."

"Elysian," Dad said. "Aunt Sazón says you were out with Lalo yesterday, so now Mom and I have to execute you."

"My Lord, Marcos!" Mom said.

"Dad," I said, giggling as Aunt Sazón huffed and walked out of my room.

"Are you counting down the time?" he asked. "Four weeks, girl. *Cuatro semanas.*"

"How have you been, sweetie?" Mom said. "Aunt Sazón is a little concerned."

"She's always concerned about anyone who doesn't act exactly like her."

"Elysian," Mom said, firmly. "She's my sister."

"I'm sorry for your tragedy."

"Hah!" Dad said. "Good one!"

"Oh, Elysian," Mom continued. They gave me a recap of their time in Buenos Aires. Mom had spent time studying artifacts from the Quilmes people. Dad had studied hair genes with other genetics professors. He could have studied anything, but he focused on why some people have brown hair instead.

"Ready for Thanksgiving?" Dad asked. "No school for a whole week."

"No. I have to eat with *certain people.*"

"Says who? Go eat with Lalo or Brandon if you want."

"Marcos, Thanksgiving is about family," Mom said.

"*Ay Diosito,*" Dad said. "Nobody likes eating with your family."

Just before I got off the phone, Dad sang more off-key than ever. It was an old song by R.E.M. called "West of the Fields," a song from their first album that came out twenty years before I was born. The lyrics have the word "Elysian," but the singer says it as "Eh-lee-shun." Dad got halfway through the song before Mom begged him to shut up. She said goodbye and promised they would be back in four weeks.

"Okay," I answered. "I'll be waiting. I need to get ready for school."

"Stay heavenly," Dad said. "I love you so much."

"I love you, too, Elysian," Mom joined in.

"Same," I said and hung up the phone. I changed into black jeans, an oversized green t-shirt, and my athletic shoes, as if I would ever run somewhere. Aunt Sazón made oatmeal and chopped fruit for breakfast. I only ate a small amount and told her I was leaving early.

"Can't wait to see Lalo, huh?" she said. She was right, but the way she said it made me leave my house quicker than usual. As I walked, Brandon texted me. He was already at school in geology tutorials. He told me he'd meet me by the vending machines in the courtyard around 8:10.

When I got to school, I saw Nate talking to Tiana. I sat close to them behind a large bush, so I could eavesdrop without them noticing.

"But she shouldn't have freaked out," I heard Nate say.

"It doesn't matter, she didn't want you to kiss her."

"Why not? Is she gay or something?"

Yes, Nate. The only reason a girl wouldn't want to kiss you is because she's gay, and not because you're a total creep.

"I don't think so," Tiana said. "I think she likes Lalo."

"Lalo? He's stupid." *Not as stupid as you, Nate.*

"He's okay," Tiana said. "He's kinda cute, not as cute as Brandon, but he's not bad. It doesn't matter though... if she doesn't like you, then she doesn't like you."

"Oh well, she's probably gay. Doesn't matter." Hell, I didn't mind at all if he thought I liked girls. It just meant I was off the hook.

"Look, there's Brandon!" Tiana said when she noticed him. "He's so HOT!"

"I can't believe you like him."

"He's *sooooooo* cute." I couldn't see her, but I could imagine the drool rolling down her chin at the sight of Brandon.

"Elysian!" Brandon called out, waving his hands. "Come over here!"

I got up and walked to him. If Lalo didn't show up soon, he'd be late. Brandon pulled out his wallet, fumbled through the pockets, and handed me an old, nearly rubbed off movie ticket stub.

"What's this for?" I asked.

"Oh, wrong thing," he said, taking it from my hand. "Hold on."

He dug through his stuffed wallet more, pulling out crumpled dollar bills, guitar picks, rewards cards for store that didn't exist anymore until he finally found what he was looking for.

"A condom?!" I yelled out. "I don't need a condom!"

"It's for protection. Aren't you and Lalo together?"

"Not like this!" I said, tossing the condom back to him. "What are you doing with that anyway? It expired two years ago."

"Man, I don't even know. I just grab stuff and put it in my wallet sometimes. Hey, where is Lalo anyway?"

"I don't know. He should be here by now."

Right as I said that, we saw him running towards us, wearing a red polo, green shorts, and a white cap with the words *CORPUS CHRISTI, TEXAS*.

"I made it," he said, out of breath with his hands on his knees. "I woke up late. Plus, my dad had an early call, so I couldn't get a ride."

"Take the cap off, we can't wear hats at school," Brandon said, yanking it off his head.

"I'll take it," I said, tossing Lalo's cap into my backpack as he caught his breath. He stood up straight and let out a big yawn, followed by a smaller yawn.

"I'm tired," he said. "Thanksgiving can't get here soon enough."

Lunch was different that day. Tiana only stopped by for a few minutes, mostly to fangirl over Brandon. Nate didn't come by at all. Brandon told me and Lalo about a kid named Billy Dobson. In 1985, he went to a creek with his best friends. When they headed home, he was with them, but by the time they got to their neighborhood, he was gone. People had been coming up with theories ever since. Billy was killed by his friends. He fell in the creek and his friends freaked out and lied about what happened to him. Aliens took him. Bigfoot ate him.

"Really?" Lalo said. "Bigfoot? Where did this happen?"

"In Texas," Brandon said. "Gun Barrel City."

"Yeah right," Lalo said. "Bigfoot would die in Texas. It's too damn hot."

"The minute aliens stepped off their spaceship in Texas, they'd hop right back on and head to the East Coast," I said. "Was Billy ever found?"

"Nope," Brandon said. "Still missing."

"Like Gladys," Lalo said with a sigh. "I think she's dead. My parents have hope. I don't."

Brandon took a quick bite out of his hamburger. "You know, of all the missing person stories I've read, hers is interesting. I bet you a hundred bucks she's alive. She's probably being kept somewhere."

"You don't know," Lalo said. "Nobody knows."

"Dude," Brandon said. "Trust me. She is."

"How do you know for sure?" Lalo asked.

"Simple," Brandon answered, taking a sip of his orange juice. "She's hot."

"Take that back!" Lalo said.

"Think about it, Lalo," Brandon said, patting him on his shoulder. "She's pretty. Why would someone kill her?"

"So, you're saying she's being tortured by some sicko?" Lalo asked.

"Possibly. She's not dead though. I swear on my dad's old Torah."

After school, I swung by Brandon's house. Mr. Meyer was there, yelling at the TV because the reporters said there would be rain on the weekend.

"Elysian!" Mr. Meyer called out. "It's going to pour!"

"What's the big problem about rain, Dad?" Brandon asked, shutting off the TV. "We need it."

"People who go clubbing don't like standing in line in the

rain," Mr. Meyer said. "They won't come out and then I'll get sent home early."

"This is why you should go to night school, Dad," Brandon said. "Or day school. Whatever. Even clown college would work."

"I haven't studied anything in over twenty years. I ain't too smart."

"Yeah, you are, Mr. Meyer," I said, sitting down across from him. "You left the only community you ever knew and made a new life for yourself. That took a lot of brain power."

"Thanks, Elysian," he said.

Brandon and I studied geology for two hours. He seemed to understand more and had enough of the key terms memorized to pass the next test. He closed his textbook and shoved it away.

"So ready for Thanksgiving," he said. "Enough of this rock shit."

"Just wait until we take chemistry in high school."

"Like you and Lalo aren't already having chemistry."

"Shut up, Brandon."

"You should tell Tiana to plan y'all's wedding."

I left for home a little after six. To my surprise, Ajo was waiting there with his girlfriend Florence. They were on the couch, making out like the next day was the end of the world. I wanted to tell them to stop, but they were being so loud, I didn't think they'd hear me.

"Okay, let's take a break," Florence said, rolling over.

"Please do," I said.

"Ella?!" Ajo cried out, standing up immediately. "What are you doing here?"

"I live here. What are you doing here?"

"My mom told me I had to be here when you got home."

"Okay," I said. "Carry on with your party."

"Who are you?" Florence asked. "You're cute."

"I'm Ajo's cousin."

"Who's Ajo?"

"I mean, Ricardo. We call him Ajo... it means garlic."

"Because I'm strong," he said, flexing his arms to her delight.

"It's because your face is strong enough to scare vampires," I whispered to myself as I walked to my bedroom. I changed into comfy clothes to lounge around in. Once I heard smooching sounds coming from the living room, I put on my phone's headset and listened to music on YouTube. I started off with The Beatles, then skipped to a band Dad liked called The Who.

I turned the music down thirty minutes later when Aunt Sazón's voice rang out. "What are you doing here alone with *my son?*"

"He invited me over!" Florence said.

"What would your parents think if they found out?" Aunt Sazón said. "Proper girls don't spend time alone with boys!"

"Ma!" Ajo squealed. "Calm down."

"I will not! She shouldn't be alone with you!"

"*¡Mamá, nada pasó!*" Ajo assured her.

"I'm getting out of here, Ricky," Florence said.

Ricky. How cute. It was better than Garlic. I heard Florence rush out the door as Aunt Sazón lectured Ajo on why Florence was the wrong woman for him to date. She told him good girls don't kiss so soon or don't dress so openly. My guess was Florence was around Ajo's age, meaning she was at least twenty. She was an adult, so she could kiss whoever she wanted, and she could damn sure wear whatever the hell she wanted.

"Ma, c'mon, she's pretty," Ajo said. "Just give her a chance."

"I will not let you get involved with a girl like her," she said.

"I bet you she can't cook. This is why we need to work on Elysian. She'll end up like Florence."

If ending up like Florence meant I'd be making out on a stranger's couch with a boy named Garlic, then I defintely needed protection.

During dinner, I ate with Aunt Sazón, Ajo, Oregano, and Canelo. Uncle Juke came by when dinner was almost done. He smelled like beer, oranges, smoke, and fried chicken.

"Hey Ella," he said with a long burp. "Only a couple more weeks until your parents are home! How are you feeling about seeing them soon?"

"I'm feeling great," I said. And I was, a little. I wished they'd save teaching abroad for when I was older and didn't need them around as much anymore. But, they always said it was good for their career and made them stand out from other professors. It made them unique compared to other people in their same fields. *But was it worth it?* "I'm going to bed," I said to everyone. "I'm tired."

"It's only eight," Aunt Sazón said. "Don't you want dessert?"

"No thanks. I'm pretty exhausted."

I went into my room, finished up the last bit of homework I had, and climbed into bed. My phone buzzed three times in a row. I thought I had texts, but the notifications were for junk emails. When I plugged in my phone to its charger, it buzzed again, this time with a text from Lalo.

Hellooooooooooo.

Yeah?

Do you know the answer to number six on our math homework?

I got -26.

What???? I got 52!

You must've dropped a negative sign somewhere.

Oh, I did. So, kiss tomorrow?

Yesssssssss Lalo, yesssssssss.

USS Defiance?

Again?

Hey, why not? Let's make out on the haunted deck he texted with six kissing face emojis.

Okay, you got a deal.

I fell asleep quickly and stayed asleep the entire night. I hadn't slept well in a while. When I woke up, my first thought wasn't "am I gonna die?" but "what's for breakfast?" From what I read about anxiety, it worked in waves. One week could be terrible and one week could be extraordinary.

The waves at Emerald Beach were like any other beach, but on certain days, especially during the mid-summer, the waves got stronger. The waves were powerful enough to wash the surfers away into the distant ocean, yet that's when some people surfed the most. We hadn't had a bad hurricane in a few years—only then were the waves stronger. The big waves were intimidating, but they always calmed down eventually.

Anxiety seemed to be just like that—big, strong, terrifying waves followed by tame, easygoing ones. I told myself to remember that, even when it was hard. As strong as anxiety could be, it hadn't hurt me. I hoped it would stay tame for a long time.

Chapter 21

The next day, the USS Defiance held a special tour called Full Hull. For thirty dollars, the tour took visitors to extra spots that weren't usually open to the public. Lalo and I hoped the tour didn't include our secret observation deck.

"If they find us, we'll make something up," he said.

"Like what?"

"We ate a lot of chili and farted so hard, we flew up to the deck."

"Lalo, that's impossible."

"C'mon, Elysian," he said, making a loud raspberry noise as everyone in the main hall turned to look at us.

"Don't draw attention. These people will think we're up to something."

"Okay. I'll keep quiet about Operation Lips-on-Lips," he said. I started laughing so hard, everyone stared at us a second time. "Quiet, you'll make everyone suspect our mission. They're gonna call the navy and have us torpedoed." He gave me a quick kiss on my cheek. It was light, soft, and over within a second, but it felt amazing.

"Where should we go first?" I asked. "This place is huge."

"Hmmm... the sailor quarters."

"Good choice." We headed to entrance three which housed

the sailor quarters, the cafeteria, and the training gym. The beds were made the way the sailors kept them back during World War II. The skinny mattresses couldn't have looked more uncomfortable. There was an intercom mounted to the wall, most likely as an alarm. I wondered how the sailors woke up for the day. Did the captain scream into the intercom or was it a long, screeching sound that could wake up the dead?

"How did they sleep on those things?" Lalo said, pointing to the skinniest mattress. "Being a sailor must have sucked."

"Someone had to do the job. I wouldn't."

"I wouldn't either. I couldn't sleep on that."

"Let's go to the deck before anyone sees us."

"Already? We just got here."

"Before it gets packed. We have to be quiet, too."

"I'll be quieter than quiet. Watch."

We walked towards entrance six, the final part of the main tour. When we reached the chapel, there were three other people inside. We sat on one of the pews while they read all the info labels.

"Operation in trouble," Lalo whispered in my ear.

"Not yet, we still have plenty of time."

"I have to pee."

"Really? Now we have to go back to the main hall."

"All right, then I'll pee in my pants."

"No, let's go. Hopefully by the time we get back, these people will be gone."

We headed to the main entrance through crowds of kids, tourists, and people on the Full Hull tour. For whatever reason, the women's restroom was by the deli, but the men's restroom was down a narrow ladder on a lower level. Lalo stretched his arms and legs, took a deep breath, and started his journey to the restroom.

"These steps are steep, I'm gonna pee myself before I get to the restroom."

"I'll be here. See you in a bit." I heard his footsteps get further away as I sat down by the top of the ladder. The floor was ice cold. I noticed it was a little sunken down, too. I didn't hear Lalo's footsteps anymore and assumed he made it to the restroom. Then, my mind took over. *Something told me he had fallen off the ladder, cracked his head open, and was down there, bleeding alone. Or maybe he made it to the restroom, but slipped and hurt himself and I wouldn't be able to get to him since I couldn't go into the men's restroom. My breathing rushed, my skin burned, my heart sprinted, and my hands and feet went numb. I rocked back and forth as even more horrible thoughts took over me like Lalo falling through a window and drowning in the ocean. He was kidnapped like Gladys. Or tripped on his shoelaces and broke his knees. Or hurt his wrists...*

"Elysian?" I heard Lalo say. I looked up and wanted to reach out to him, but my hands tingled and it was extremely hard to move them. Lalo sat next to me and wrapped an arm around me. "Breathe... breathe iiiiiiiiiin, breathe ooooooooout."

"I can't," I said, almost out of breath. "So scared."

"What are you scared of?"

"I thought you got hurt."

"Me? No way. I don't get hurt. I get grazed."

"Where's Gladys?" I asked.

"I don't know. I think she's in a nice, upbeat place. I bet she's taking photos and videos of clouds and putting them on whatever websites they got in the afterlife. Heavengram. Cloudbook. Angelchat. YouDead."

"My mind told me you fell down and hurt your head."

"Maybe I need a good head pounding. It would probably make me better at math. Are you scared of anything else?"

"I want my parents. They're always gone."

"They'll be home soon," he said, patting my shoulder. "What else? C'mon, tell me everything. We got lots of time."

"I don't know... dying. The dark. Roaches. My uncle hitting me again. My aunt nagging me until I combust. Being alone. Being unloved."

"Your uncle will never hurt you again, I promise. As for your aunt, she talks a lot. But she's all words and no action. Roaches got roach spray. The dark is temporary. The sun always comes up. And you are loved. I'm not sure what love feels like, but I like you a whole lot. I guess love is liking someone so much, you'd do anything for them."

"I feel better," I said, breathing a little smoother. "Deck?"

"Not until you're completely better. Whenever you are, then we'll go."

"I can go up there now."

"Are you a hundred percent sure?" Lalo asked, rubbing my back with his hand.

I had feeling in my hands and feet again. My heart rate was back to normal. My breathing was slower. The big wave calmed down. "Yeah," I said.

"Okay," he said, helping me stand. "But if you feel like we need to leave or you need a break, tell me."

"I will, I promise."

We walked back to entrance six and the crowd seemed even larger than earlier. The odds of us having the chapel to ourselves looked slim. We counted twelve people, all of them reading the info labels. They appeared distracted enough not to notice us.

"Wanna sneak up there?" I whispered to Lalo.

"Up that steeper than hell ladder?"

"You're fast, you can get up there."

"Let's just wait a tiny bit longer."

We sat quietly on a pew, observing each person's move. A few more people entered the chapel, but didn't stay for long. Eventually, we were the only ones left. We rushed up the ladder before that changed.

"I thought we'd never get up here," Lalo said. "Did everyone and their grandma decide to visit the USS Defiance today?"

"I hope no one saw us," I said, scooting next to him.

"No, I don't think anyone did. They would have reported us by now."

"If we get caught, do you think we could get banned?"

"Banned? I doubt it. We're just kids," he said with a shrug. "You ready? Be honest with me."

"I'm ready."

He leaned in closer to me, pressed his lips against mine, and kissed me gently. I did the same to him. He slowly slipped his tongue into my mouth. It was obvious he doused his mouth with minty mouthwash sometime earlier in the day. We kissed each other a little bit stronger.

Lalo reached a hand up and patted my hair. "Still okay?" he asked.

"I am."

"If you need me to stop, raise your hand and I will."

"I'm fine." We kissed a while longer, until his phone went off with a text from Brandon. Mine buzzed with the same text, too.

Dudes! Call!

"Should we?" I asked. "We're kinda busy."

"I guess we should. Want me to go down first?"

"Yeah, go ahead." He took a deep breath, cleared his throat, and headed down. For some reason, I heard cheers and people shouting. The noise covered up our sneaking around, but I couldn't figure out why everyone else was being so loud. I thought back to when we were at the main entrance. I hadn't seen any signs about a special event. Lalo was safely at the bottom of the ladder within a minute. It was my turn next. The ladder felt a little less narrow than usual and I was able to make it down in record time.

"I don't know what's going on," Lalo said. "Everybody is rushing somewhere. Is the ship on fire? Did we miss something?"

"We would've heard an alarm." Anxiety was telling me there was an alarm we didn't hear, but my rational mind told me that alarms were meant to be heard.

"Whatever is going on, I wanna check it out," he said.

"No!" I said, pulling on his arm. "We might be in trouble."

"Us? No way. Everybody would be running towards us if we were. Let's look and if it's bad, we can just leave. Deal?"

"Deal," I said, following him. We walked quickly to where everyone else was going. People zoomed past us as we looked straight ahead, making sure we headed to the right spot. When we reached the main entrance, we saw at least fifty police officers marching through the crowd while the others spoke into their cellphones or radios. My jaw clenched and my mind spiraled. I thought another attack was coming. Lalo noticed and told me everything was going to be okay.

"How do you know?" I asked.

"All these cops are here. Whatever's going on, they can handle it."

My phone buzzed ten times in a row and all ten texts were from Brandon.

DUDES!!!!!!

CALL ME!!!

Now!

What the hell????

Y'all STILL making out???

Stop it!

C'mon dudes, take a break!

C-A-L-L ME.

I'm serious!!!!

Hey, here's an idea. CALL ME!

I tried calling, but more and more texts kept coming, causing my phone to crash. Lalo's phone did the same. We restarted them, waiting with sweat coming from our foreheads for them to reset. Mine was ready first, so I made the call.

"What's going on?" I asked as soon as Brandon answered.

"Finally! Gladys is alive!"

"What? She's alive?"

"Gladys is alive?" Lalo cried out.

"It's on the news," Brandon said. "She was being held prisoner on the USS Defiance. Someone found her during a tour, a new one, Full Hull or something. But anyway, she's alive!"

"Where's my sister?!" Lalo yelled, running up to an officer. I got off the phone with Brandon and went to Channel 4 RCIN's website. It was breaking news.

GLADYS RICHARDSON FOUND ALIVE!
DETAILS TO FOLLOW

My mind said the news was wrong and the real Gladys was lying in a grave somewhere, but I knew the reality.

"I can see her later," Lalo said, his voice breaking a little.

"She's going to the hospital to get checked out. She's alive. She's really alive."

"Do you wanna stay here or do you wanna go home?" I asked. "Your parents must want you home."

"Oh yeah, I guess. Let's roll."

As we walked, Lalo called his parents, but Mrs. Richardson's phone was off. She usually slept until seven in the evening before she had to be up for work. Mr. Richardson's phone was on, but going straight to voicemail, so Lalo texted them instead.

"I bet Dad has a heavy job. And there's no way Mom is gonna wake up until I get home and scream," he said. "Elysian, I have a sister again!"

"You do! I wonder what happened. Why would someone abduct her just to keep her on the island?"

"Hell, I don't know. Must've been a real idiot. USS Defiance wasn't a bad idea though, it's big and a lot of parts are off limits to the public. It's not a shabby place to hide someone. But seriously, what the hell?"

"I'm sure Brandon will have it all figured out within the next couple hours. I have no idea how he knew she was alive."

"He reads enough about this kind of stuff to know," Lalo said.

"We'll know soon enough." We reached his house and found it swamped with reporters. Mrs. Richardson stepped outside with messy hair, still in her pajamas.

"WHAT THE HELL IS THIS?" she screamed. "GET OFF MY PROPERTY!"

"Mom! No!" Lalo said, hurrying to her. "Gladys is alive! Someone found her!"

Mrs. Richardson was silent for a minute and then let out a scream of joy. I waved bye to Lalo and Mrs. Richardson and headed home. Aunt Sazón was there with her eyes focused on the TV. Reporter after reporter talked about Gladys and shots of the USS Defiance were shown over and over again.

"Imagine," Aunt Sazón said, shaking her head. "She was on that ship this entire time. All those sightings were worthless."

"I wouldn't say they were worthless. People were trying to help."

"What good is the help if it leads nowhere?"

"I mean, it's better than nothing. I'm glad she's fine. I thought she was dead."

"Everyone did. And this whole time, she was right on the island."

I went outside to check the mail. It was mostly junk, coupons for places Mom and Dad occasionally visited, menus for new restaurants in the area, and academic journals Mom and Dad subscribed to but never read. I saw a letter from Oxford University addressed to Drs. Lecaro. Mom made it clear to everyone she wasn't Mrs. Lecaro, but Dr. Lecaro as well. Even though the letter wasn't for me, I tore it open anyway.

Drs. Lecaro,

We have heard immense stories about your teaching skills. Each of you are superior experts in your fields. We would be honoured if you would teach at Oxford for a one-year fellowship. Please let us know by the 8ᵗʰ of January. We look forward to your response.

—Oxford Administration

I stuck the letter in my pocket and went inside. I placed the mail on the kitchen table, and snuck away to Mom and Dad's office while Aunt Sazón was still busy watching TV. Once inside, I shut the door behind me. I turned on their paper shredder and jammed the Oxford letter inside, watching it become hundreds of little pieces. Mom and Dad had talked about Oxford University a lot and had even visited before, but never for more than a couple days. They spoke about wanting to teach there sometime in the future. I was sure they would be invited again eventually. But for now, they didn't need to know.

Chapter 22

When Gladys was ready for visitors, Lalo told me I could come to his house to see her. She was much thinner than before. Her hair was matted, her skin was paler, and her eyes were sunken like she hadn't slept in years.

"Elysian," she said. "Hi doll."

"Hey," I said, slowly sitting next to her at the kitchen table. My mind told me this wasn't the real Gladys, but someone pretending to be her. That she was actually dead and this was just a dream. It didn't make any sense, but my mind convinced me.

"So, what happened?"

"Oh gosh," she said, rolling her eyes and running a hand through her long, black hair. "What didn't happen?"

"Who abducted you?"

"Two men. Both had nicknames. One was Stereo, the other was Loudmouth. No idea who they were. They used to work at the USS Defiance. They had keys to a room in the lower area, where they were holding me."

"I'm gonna kill them!" Lalo said, waving his fists around. "With my bare hands!"

"Lalito, you're just a baby! My little baby brother."

"Why am I your baby brother?" he said with his eyes fluttering. Their old joke was coming and, after so long, I was excited to hear it.

"You're my baby brother because you're younger than me and you're a boy."

"And you're my big sister because you're older and you're a lady," he said.

"That's right," she said, hugging him. "You will always be my baby brother."

"Did they torture you?" I asked Gladys.

"They tried," she said. "They also tried doing something... *horrible* to me, but I used my longest nail to jab at their eyes and they never tried again."

"I'm so glad you're okay," I said. "Do you mind if I give you a hug?"

"Sure," she said, opening her arms. "Thank you for asking me first."

I hugged her and Lalo joined us. My mind repeated that this wasn't Gladys again, but I knew it was because if this wasn't Gladys, Lalo wouldn't have hugged her along with me.

After visiting Gladys, I walked to Brandon's house. He was out front, lying on his lawn with his eyes closed. I screamed, thinking something was wrong.

"What's going on?" he asked, confused.

"What the hell are you doing? I thought you were dead."

"Yes Elysian, Brandon is dead. I am his spirit. Brandon's final wish was for you to get him ice cream, because it's November and still as hot as Satan's butthole."

"Get up, Brandon."

He groaned and stood up, stretching his arms to the sky and popping his back. "My dad is freaked out. I just came out to get some peace and quiet for a few minutes."

"Why? What happened?"

"He's losing weight. He's on a low-fat, low-carb, high-protein diet, so he's going wacko. He wants to eat junk but our house is full of grilled chicken, fish, turkey, and vegetables."

"Oh man, he's on a diet and Thanksgiving is in five days? That's gonna suck."

"We're eating at Lalo's. I told him if he eats any desserts, I'm gonna call my grandparents and tell them he's coming home to be a rabbi."

"Your dad as a rabbi?" I asked, laughing.

"He was gonna be a rabbi like my grandpa before he ran away. That's why it's bad. He ran away from becoming a rabbi, girl. If he had been a regular dude running away, maybe they wouldn't talk to him, but at least they wouldn't treat him like he didn't exist."

"He makes a better bouncer anyway."

"Yeah, totally. Wanna go to Retro World or something? I'm hungry. I have enough money for both of us."

"Sure, let's go."

"Okay, let me tell Dad," he said, walking to his front door. He slightly opened it and called out, "Dad! Going to get something to eat with Elysian!"

"GOOD GOD, I WANT A COOKIE!" I heard Mr. Meyer answer. "THE BIGGEST!"

Brandon and I skipped Retro World and ended up at a little café called Captain Jack's instead. It had been open for a couple years, but we had never gone there. The prices were cheap as long as we only got appetizers.

"This place is too much," Brandon said. "Twelve bucks for a burger?"

"Retro World is just one block over."

"Yeah, but it's hot. I don't wanna walk back out there."

"Then garlic knots and marinara sauce it is."

"Fancy schmancy. We're like those rich tourists."

Unfortunately, the garlic knots were dry and the marinara sauce was watered down. Brandon paid with a crumpled ten dollar bill and tipped with eight quarters.

"This place sucks," he said. "Let's get out of here."

"Where do you wanna go now?"

"Hell, I don't know. We can try my house, if my dad isn't throwing more tantrums."

We walked back to his house where Mr. Meyer was screaming about the cauliflower rice he was eating. "This tastes like the stuff Satan makes you for dinner once you reach hell."

"Dad, it can't be that bad," Brandon said.

"Easy for you to say. You don't have to eat it."

Brandon and I spent an hour watching the news. The two guys who abducted Gladys were on the run. They were also suspected of committing the Emerald Beach Shooting. Gladys told the police they had guns and since she was abducted around the same time, it made sense for one of them to have caused the diversion. There was no telling though.

"They are guilty," Brandon said. "I'm one thousand percent sure."

"You can't know for sure," I said. "You're not investigating what happened."

"Dude, I just *know*. You wanna abduct someone in a public place, you need to divert attention somewhere else so you can get your abduction done."

"You sound like you could commit the perfect crime."

"Yeah man, I totally could," he answered, nodding. "If you

ever wanna murder someone, remember to wear shoes that are bigger than your real size, so the footprints won't match. You should also leave another person's hair at the scene, so the DNA will never trace back to you."

"Good Lord, Brandon. Don't say that out in public."

Before I left Brandon's house, he showed me pictures of his grandparents, Rabbi and Mrs. Meyer. They looked about sixty. Rabbi Meyer had a long, dark gray beard and Mrs. Meyer wore large glasses and a cute, navy blue hat. They looked like any other sweet, senior couple; they didn't seem like people who would disown family members. I noticed Brandon had his grandfather's eyes. Their eyes were mixed hues of blue and green, like the water at Emerald Beach. Rabbi Meyer was missing out. His grandson not only had his eyes, but deep knowledge, too. It didn't matter that the knowledge was about murder mysteries or missing person cases, because Brandon definitely knew more than the average forensic scientist.

Mr. and Mrs. Richardson and Lalo missed Gladys so much when she was gone. The entire island missed her. People far away from Rey Carlos thought they saw her and called the police to report their sightings. Brandon's grandparents knew exactly where he lived. They knew they had a grandson, but they didn't care.

"These dudes are gonna die without ever meeting me," Brandon said. "Whatever."

"It's not right," I said.

"It is to them."

"Doesn't mean it's right."

He shrugged. "They can believe what they want."

I said bye to Mr. Meyer and he grumbled about having to get ready for work. He didn't appear to have new cuts or bruises on him for once. When I started walking out the door, I heard him and Brandon talking about Rabbi and Mrs. Meyer.

"Ain't it a riot?" I heard Mr. Meyer say. "My dad's a religious guy and doesn't give a shiiiiiit about his son or his grandson."

"Maybe he'll change his mind someday," I said. "Bye, guys."

"Bye Elysian!" Mr. Meyer said. "Next time you come over, bring cookies!"

When I got home, Dad called and asked about Gladys.

"She's fine. She lost a ton of weight. She'll be back to a hundred percent soon. Everyone is happy to have her home."

"That's wonderful, Elysian. If you ever went missing, I don't know what Mom and I would do."

It was sweet to hear, but hard to believe. *How would he ever know I was missing if he barely saw me?*

"Mom says hi, she's busy finishing a new project for her department. This university is incredible. The students are brilliant. The professors are geniuses. This is an amazing school, Elysian. If you ever wanna go here for college, let me and Mom know and we'll make arrangements."

"My Spanish isn't so great," I reminded him. "How am I gonna go to school in a country where everyone speaks perfect Spanish?"

"*Por favor*," he said. "I learned Spanish and English. You can learn, too. Learning a language is not the toughest task in the world." He had a point. Being Otavalo Ecuadorian, Dad grew up speaking Kichwa, a dialect of the Quechua language. He didn't learn Spanish until high school and learned English in college along with Mom.

"Yeah, but you're a super genius. I'm not."

"Elysian, *mi cielo*. You, my daughter, are very smart. You are part of me and part of Mom. You can learn how to make your

Spanish shine like your precious eyes, *hijita*. Believe in yourself, girl."

"I will, Dad. I love you."

"I love you, too, my heaven. *Mi niña tan linda.*"

"Okay, Dad," I said. "Tell Mom I love her. I think Aunt Sazón is about to serve dinner. I can smell something."

"You got it, Elysian. Talk soon."

He hung up first as I made my way out to the kitchen and saw Aunt Sazón pulling roasted chicken breasts out of the oven. She placed the hot casserole dish on one of the stove burners and fanned herself with a newspaper. "You hungry?" she asked.

"No, not much."

"I'm not either. If you want, I can wrap this up and you can take it to school for lunch tomorrow. What do you think?"

"Sure, thanks," I said, twirling a strand of hair with my finger. "And you know, I'm sorry for all the times I've been kinda mean to you."

"It's fine. You just take after your mother." I wanted to tell her to take her opinion and stick it down her throat, but I didn't.

Once night fell, I stayed in bed, wide awake for a long time. I tried playing soothing music on my phone, but it didn't help. My mind told me Gladys would be kidnapped again, and this time, she wouldn't come home. Brandon's grandparents were plotting against him. Mom and Dad decided they liked Buenos Aires so much, they would never, ever come home. Lalo only kissed me because he wanted the "one thing all boys want." I folded my pillow and rested my head. I kept my eyes closed as tightly as I could. I tried the soothing music one more time. Nothing worked. By four in the morning, I got up and went to the kitchen to make myself a peanut butter and jelly sandwich. Once I finished eating, I washed my plate with a little stream of water and made sure the plate didn't touch the inside of the kitchen sink. Even with my efforts, Aunt Sazón still heard me.

"Awake?" she asked from the guest bedroom.

"Couldn't sleep!"

"Did you count sheep?" she asked. I don't know how someone came up with the idea of counting sheep. Why sheep? How come we don't count hippos or camels? "Get back to bed. You need sleep before school."

"I'll be fine," I said. I heard her shuffling around and before I could escape the kitchen, she had joined me.

"Did you make a snack?"

"A peanut butter and jelly sandwich."

"There's no nutrition in that. You need to learn how to cook soon."

"Here we go," I whispered to myself.

"Go back to sleep and I'll make you a good, nutritious breakfast. Eggs, sausage, whatever you want."

"Okay, I will." I wasn't sleepy, but I wanted to get away from her. I hopped back in bed with the covers over me and my pillow under my head, even though I knew I wasn't going to get any more sleep.

At five in the morning, my phone buzzed with a text from Lalo.
Up?
Yeah. I didn't sleep.
Did you count sheep?
Where would I count sheep? I don't live on a farm.
Yeah, you're right. Hey, are we a THING?
What?
You know. Are you my girlfriend?
I don't know, you haven't asked me to be.
Oh yeah, hold on.

A couple minutes later, his name flashed across the screen. He spoke in a low voice, so I assumed he was the only one awake in his house. "Elysian Lecaro... wait, don't you have a middle name? I forgot."

"Nope."

"Okay, so... Elysian Lecaro, will you be my girlfriend? I didn't want to ask you over text."

"Are you sure, Lalo?"

"Elysian, I hate talking on the phone. I'm sure."

"Even with my anxiety? My attacks? My worries? My heavy breathing? My fears? Are you sure you want me to be your girlfriend? There's something wrong with me."

"Something is wrong with everyone. But I like you. I like you a whole lot. I know you have anxiety and I know you have attacks. And I still like you."

"But why?"

"Because I know who you are when you're not anxious."

My chest suddenly felt warm and my face flushed. "Why are you so sweet?"

"Well, I did eat ice cream earlier. I'm full of sugar."

"I'll be your girlfriend."

"You will?" he said. "AWESOME!"

"Be quiet, you'll wake up the whole neighborhood."

"Man, I don't even *caaaaaaaaare!*"

Chapter 23

I spent the day before Thanksgiving with Lalo. We stopped by Pastry Pete's for hot chocolate and cookies. Tiana was there helping her parents work the register. When she got a moment to herself, she sat with us to tell us how cute we looked.

"I can't believe I never picked up on y'all's chemistry!" she said. "It was in my face the whole time!"

"How's Nate?" Lalo asked.

"Oh, he's Nate. I don't really talk to him a lot anymore. So when's y'all's wedding?!?!? We need to start planning!"

"Tiana, we just started dating."

"So? Everyone's different. My parents got engaged after three months together. How long did your parents date?"

I had no idea. I knew they got married in 2001, but I didn't know what year they met. "I don't know," I told her. I wouldn't have been surprised if their first date was talking about theories. Maybe Dad proposed to Mom in his final thesis.

"What about your parents, Lalo?" she asked, her lips smacking.

"Uhm, I don't know either," he said, taking a bite of his cookie. "They got married in 1994, I think. My mom said she was doing a nursing internship at a hospital and my dad went to the ER with a paperclip stuck in his nose. Not a very romantic story, huh?"

"It's cute!" Tiana said, running her tongue over her lips like she was about to eat something delicious. "I love romantic stories!"

"Hey, me and Elysian need to go home and fold towels," Lalo said. "Right, Elysian?"

"Oh yeah. It's gonna take a long time."

"Aw, that sucks," Tiana said. "I love hanging out with you guys!"

We left Pastry Pete's before Tiana could distract us into staying longer. As we walked home, Lalo texted Gladys to ask her how she was doing. She immediately texted back *Still at home. Love you.* We weren't sure when or if she'd ever move back to her apartment with Octavio. I had only seen him come around once to see Gladys.

"Are you coming over for Thanksgiving?" Lalo asked.

"I dunno. I'm supposed to eat with my family, but I'm not looking forward to it."

"Brandon and his dad are coming. So is Octavio, I think. And my grandparents, too. Ask your parents if you can come over."

"Why? They're in Argentina."

"Yeah, but they overrule your aunt. Right?"

"Well yeah, I guess they do."

When I got home, Aunt Sazón was splashing white wine all over a raw turkey. Some of the wine splashed off the turkey and into her eyes. She muttered something to herself, but I couldn't hear what she said. There were dishes of roasted potatoes, green beans, mixed vegetables, buttered rice, and dinner rolls on every counter, plus what smelled like a sweet dessert baking in the oven.

"Why is there so much food?" I asked.

"I have a house full of boys and a brother coming over. Men eat a lot."

"Can't they come over and help you?"

"What? No way, men can't cook."

"They can't? Are they allergic to the kitchen?"

"Ella," she said, rubbing wine off her face. "They're not built for cooking. Us women know how to work a kitchen."

"My dad cooks."

"Your dad is something else. He's not your average man."

Instead of talking more, I went to the pantry, grabbed a granola bar, and walked away as quickly as I could.

"Where you are going?" Aunt Sazón asked.

"My room."

"The day before Thanksgiving? Not a chance. Come in here and help with the food. You need to learn."

"I thought the food was done?"

"No! The green beans need to be seasoned and the rice needs a little more butter. Get back here and help me out."

I shuffled my feet to the kitchen. Aunt Sazón lived up her nickname. She seasoned everything with a variety of flavors. Even the butter we put in the rice had mixed seasonings. By the time we were done, it was almost seven. I sat down at the kitchen table for a break to finally eat my granola bar.

"What are you doing?" she asked.

"Taking a breather."

"We need to decorate the desserts."

"Desserts? You made more than one?"

"You didn't notice?" She walked to the kitchen island and pulled paper towels off a few baking dishes. There were brownies, two pies, two cakes, and chocolate chip cookies. She opened the refrigerator and handed me three giant cans of frosting.

"You can't be serious."

"I am," Aunt Sazón said, shrugging her shoulders. "Hungry men need their food."

"Can't decorating wait until later?"

"It's best to do it now. The frosting will harden and the flavor will be stronger by tomorrow."

"All right," I said, standing up. I used a rubber spatula to scoop the frosting from the cans and rubbed it generously on each cake. I couldn't tell what flavor the cakes were. When I thought I was done with Aunt Sazón's all-important cake decor, she stopped me and pointed out the spots that needed more frosting, spots where the frosting was a little drippy, and spots that had too much frosting.

"Sorry, I didn't notice," I said, rolling my eyes.

"The first time I decorated a cake, I had the same problems. You'll get it. Soon, you'll be baking cakes for Lalo."

I couldn't picture Lalo asking me for a cake, but if he did, he wasn't getting one that was picture perfect either. I did my best to fix the cakes and while they looked nicer, I didn't see why it was such a big deal. All my family members would do was eat and say nothing about how good the food was. They wouldn't help with doing the dishes or taking out the trash either. If they weren't grateful, what was the point in making sure their food looked pretty?

"What time are we eating tomorrow?" I asked.

"Five. Why?"

"Would it be okay if I swung by Lalo's before? I won't eat anything."

"Hmm, that should be fine. What time is theirs?"

"Early, like at noon. His mom has to work at six."

"Bring him over to ours. If it's okay with his parents."

"Oh... I'll ask," I said, even though I didn't want to. Lalo deserved a nice Thanksgiving, not one with a bunch of ogres sitting around eating and talking smack. I texted him later that night to ask what he thought. He took a while to text back.

I mean, I wouldn't go if you weren't there.

You think I wanna go? At least when my parents are in town, they can do most of the talking for me.

I'll go. Do you want me to bring anything?

Just yourself.

Okay, I'll be there. But please don't make me talk too much.

I won't. Promise.

The next day, I woke up at nine in the morning. I took a bubble bath and styled my hair with some help from YouTube.

Aunt Sazón was in the kitchen, taste testing the food. "Uuuuu-uuuuugh," she said, after taking a small bite of one of the dinner rolls and brushing more butter on their tops before shoving them back in the oven.

"That bad, huh?" I asked.

"Horrible. My family would ridicule me."

"Isn't that what they do best?" I said to myself.

"What time are you leaving for Lalo's?" she asked, her eyes dead set on the rest of the food. "I think I can manage whatever is left to do."

"Around 11:30. I should be home by four."

"Not any later. Did your parents call?"

"No. It's just a regular day over there, why would they?"

"Oh, yes, I completely forgot. Have a good time with your boyfriend. Make sure you offer to serve him his plate of food. Men loved being served."

"I'll keep that in mind, Aunt Sazón," I said, rolling my eyes as soon as I turned away from her. I went to my room to change into the clothes I usually wore whenever Mom and Dad had a special event to attend. Aside from super elaborate dresses, I didn't have many choices. I went through my closet and settled on a nice navy blouse and a black skirt I hadn't worn in ages. I thought about putting on a little makeup since Mom had plenty stored away in the home office. I YouTubed makeup tutorials to see if I could mimic any of them, but I couldn't. I didn't know what mascara was or what the hell foundation was or what color of blush I needed, so I closed out the app on my phone and told myself Lalo would have to enjoy my new look, whether he wanted to or not.

"Wow!" Aunt Sazón said when I stepped out of my room. "You look like a girl!"

"Thanks. Rumor has it I am one."

"No, I mean, you look *feminine*. There you go, Ella. Boys love girly girls."

"Awesome. Lalo will be so swoon, he'll pass out and hibernate until Christmas."

"That's the spirit!" Aunt Sazón said.

As I walked to Lalo's house, Brandon texted me. He had theories about why Gladys was abducted and how Octavio was involved. After the tenth text, I replied, *I'm walking to Lalo's, I can't walk and text at the same time.*

Oh man. Food's at noon, right?

Yeah.

Dude, I forgot. I'm gonna get ready right now!

Just before I got to Lalo's, Tiana texted me *Happy Thanksgiving* with tons of heart, turkey, and fall leaf emojis. I texted her back with a simple *TY.*

Have fun at LALO'S!!!!! Get it, girl! I had no idea what she meant, so I didn't respond. I rang the doorbell and Mr. Richardson swung the door open. He stood on a ladder with one hand inside the vent over the door frame.

"Elysian!" he said. "Food's ready, I think. Hold on." He stood on his tiptoes, poised his mouth right where the vent grille would usually be and shouted, "HEY GLORIA! ¿Y LA COMIDA?"

"Quit using that dang vent to talk to me, you blockhead! You keep scaring me half to death!" I heard Mrs. Richardson say. "Yes, it's ready!"

Lalo was in the kitchen helping Gladys set the table. She wore a dark blue blouse, a long, black skirt, red lipstick and teal eyeshadow.

"Hey," she said with a wink. "We're matching."

"Whoa," Lalo said when he noticed my outfit. "Are you going to a funeral? Who died?"

"You're about to die if you don't apologize," I said.

"You look nice," he said. "But it's only Thanksgiving. What gives? The turkey is what gets, uh, dressed up!"

"Lalito, you need to work on your flirting," Gladys said.

The doorbell rang and in walked Lalo's grandparents. Grandpa and Grandma Richardson had come from Corpus Christi and Grandpa and Grandma Espinosa had driven all the way from Dallas. Lalo gave the four of them loads of hugs.

"This is my girlfriend," he said, tugging at my arm. "Her name is Elysian and she's super smart. Isn't she pretty?"

"You're beautiful," Grandma Espinosa said, shaking my hand and giving me a quick kiss on my cheek.

"Lalo, aren't you too young for a girlfriend?" Grandma Richardson asked, wiping her gray bangs away from her eyes.

"Denise, you're too old for a husband, and yet, here we are," Grandpa Richardson mumbled as Grandma Richardson pinched him on his cheek.

Grandpa Espinosa, on the other hand, was fairly quiet. He spoke better Spanish than English. I greeted him in the best Spanish I knew and his face sparkled like Christmas lights. "*Gracias, niña*," he said. "*Eres muy bella.*"

Before we ate, Mr. Richardson said grace in an extremely nontraditional way. He placed a napkin halfway in his shirt collar and burped. "Thank you, Lord, for this food, for our son, and for our daughter. We ask you to ease our digestion of the beans, so we won't blow up the house with our gas. We also ask your assistance in finding the SOB who abducted Gladys and the SOB who shot Lalo and everyone else at the beach. Strike them down good, Lord, and may they burn in hell for their actions. Thank you. Amen."

"Oliver, you can't use potty language in a prayer," Grandma Richardson said. "Especially with children in the room."

"Oh, everyone knows Oliver's mouth is dirtier than the movies Elysian's uncle watches," Mrs. Richardson said with a sigh. I laughed along with Lalo and Gladys.

When I was halfway done eating, Brandon and Mr. Meyer came over. They brought a box of toaster pastries and a case of bottled water. To my surprise, Mr. Meyer had a skull cap on. I had seen him with one in his photos from his past life, but never in person.

"Mr. Meyer?" I said. "Are you okay?"

"Fine. I didn't have time to comb my hair, so this little thing is covering up the bad parts. Bet you thought I went back to Judaism. Hah!"

At two in the afternoon, Lalo, Brandon, and I went for a walk. The temperature had dipped a little, making the weather extra nice.

"Octavio didn't show up," Lalo said. "Pitiful. Gladys is alive and he's out of the picture. What a loser."

"He's not working, is he?" Brandon asked. "Retro World might be open, maybe."

"Everything is closed today except the hospital," I said. "Who knows where he is? Are they getting divorced?"

"I don't think so," Lalo said. "Gladys would have told us. I wonder what his problem is."

"He had something to do with her abduction," Brandon said.

"He wouldn't have been dumb enough to say *'yeah dudes, hide her in the USS Defiance, a ship that's literally docked onto Rey Carlos Island,'*" I said.

"Man, you haven't watched the documentaries I have," Brandon said. "Then again, I could be wrong. I hope I'm wrong."

"You are more wrong than pineapple on pizza," Lalo said. "We'll find out who took her and why soon enough."

"What about who shot us? We haven't found that out yet either," Brandon said.

"I don't even care anymore," Lalo said. "No one died. We're all fine. Gladys is fine. I'm not gonna fight whoever shot up the beach."

I got home in time to help Aunt Sazón transfer all the food from my house to hers. We loaded everything in her trunk and drove down the five houses that separated my house from hers. She unlocked the door when we arrived and we carried each pot and casserole dish one by one into the kitchen. Dirty dishes were piled in the sink, the trash bin was overflowing, and the dining table was sticky with some kind of residue.

"These silly boys," she said when we were done bringing the food inside. "They need me so much."

"Are you kidding? They can't wash dishes, take out the trash, or wipe the table? Are they that stupid?"

"Ella! They're boys! They have no idea how to keep a clean house. That's where we come in. They need us."

"Oh, barf all over that idea."

"Watch it, Elly. Lalo might not like your fiery attitude." It was too late. He already knew about it and he still liked me.

During dinner, nobody said much. Lalo showed up a minute or two after Aunt Sazón said grace. He sat next to me, lightly squeezed my hands, and announced: "Elysian is wonderful. She makes my heart jump." No one answered him. Uncle Pico kept his eyes on his plate and even when he was done eating, he kept his eyes on the tablecloth. Oregano ate two hearty servings, Ajo ate three, but Canelo barely ate anything.

"I hate this food, Mom!" Canelo cried out. "I want chicken nuggets!"

"Canelo, I spent an entire day making this food," Aunt Sazón said. "Eat at least half of what's on your plate for me, please?"

"No!" he said, pushing his plate aside and rushing to the kitchen. "I'm gonna make myself chicken nuggets!"

"Are they always like this?" Lalo whispered in my ear.

"Oh yeah. And Uncle Juke isn't even here yet."

Uncle Juke came over right after Canelo was back at the table munching on his nuggets, smelling like beer and cigarette smoke.

"Thank you for this food," he said to Aunt Sazón with grease running down from his mouth to his untamed chest hair. "It's delicious."

"You're welcome," she said. "Do you want more, Pico?"

"No," he said, his eyes still looking away. "I'm full."

"So, Lalo," Aunt Sazón said. "Doesn't Elysian look nice today?"

"She always looks nice," Lalo said. "She could wear a paper bag as a dress and still look absolutely gorgeous."

I blushed as Aunt Sazón's face turned red and her eyes squinted. Lalo reached under the table and patted my cold knee. I couldn't wait to kiss him again.

After dinner, I went back home with Aunt Sazón and Canelo. It wasn't too late in Buenos Aires, so I called Dad, but he didn't answer. I called Mom next and she picked up. "Elysian! Happy Thanksgiving!"

"Thanks Mom. How's Buenos Aires?"

"It's been a lot of fun. But Dad and I are ready to come home."

"Where is he? I called him first."

"He's fast asleep. He's been researching several hours a day for the last two weeks with other professors. They're going to wrap up in time for the end of semester."

"Oh. If they don't finish on time, will you need to stay longer?"

"No, they'll finish. Nobody wants to work past the end of the semester. We'll be home very soon. Keep being our best girl. We love you."

In the night, I lied in bed, wide awake for the thousandth time in a row. By the time I felt drowsy, the sun shined in the sky.

Chapter 24

The day my parents came home, Aunt Sazón told me I didn't need to go to school. Since final exams were coming, I wanted to go, but I knew I could easily make up the work later. I got into Aunt Sazón's car a little after nine in the morning. The drive to Dwight D. Eisenhower Airport usually took about an hour because of constant traffic in the area. Their flight would be coming into Terminal F, also known as Terminal Failure, because it was all the way on the other side of the airport and it was always hard to park there. Surprisingly, Aunt Sazón found a parking spot in less than five minutes.

"What time does their flight land?" I asked as we walked to the Terminal F doors.

"Eleven," she said. "Their flight number is 0256. Gate 31."

I sat with Aunt Sazón on a bench close to the airport coffee shop. I tried focusing on the flight screen, so I could see the exact moment when their flight landed, but the noises sidetracked me. The sounds of the blender, people ordering, the baristas working the cash register, and the endless airport announcements were especially distracting.

"I'm gonna take a walk," I said to Aunt Sazón.

"By yourself?"

"Sure."

"I don't think so. Not in a big place like this."

We walked around the entire airport, people watching and stopping occasionally inside the small gift shops to see what they had for sale. A store called Sandy Shore sold seashells for six bucks apiece. Emerald Beach had free seashells. Who were these scammers?

"Are you hungry? Thirsty?" Aunt Sazón asked when it was close to eleven in the morning. "I think I'm going to get myself a little something."

"I could use a drink." We headed to the airport food court and got in line at a place called Drinks Up whose logo was a drink cup next to a surfboard. Aunt Sazón got a strawberry slush and I got a mango lemonade, but it was so sweet, I couldn't drink most of it.

"Flight 0256 has landed," the airport announcer said. "Gate 31. Flight 0256, Buenos Aires. Once again, Flight 0256, Buenos Aires has landed."

The minute I heard the announcement, I ran to Gate 31 as Aunt Sazón dragged on behind me. She told me to slow down, but now that my parents were home, she wasn't the boss of me anymore. I reached the waiting area for Gate 31 way before she did as passengers walked out two by two. Some looked exhausted, others looked sad, and some looked happy. Finally, Mom and Dad appeared, hand in hand with their big backpacks stuffed to the max. Dad was wearing his elegant navy blue suit, as if he had just finished a presentation right before the flight. Mom was dressed more casual in a nice blouse, black slacks, and wedge heels.

"Mom! Dad!" I sprinted to them and they hugged me tightly. Dad was wearing his signature cologne and Mom had on her usual perfume. I could see them, feel them, hear them, and smell them. That's when I was sure they were really home.

"*Mi vida*," Dad said, his smooth black hair tied back in his trademark ponytail. "We missed you so much."

"How are you?" Mom asked. "You look beautiful!"

Aunt Sazón finally caught up to us. She gave Mom a quick hug and shook Dad's hand.

"I told you to slow down, Ella," Aunt Sazón said.

"*Déjala en paz*," Dad said. "Your babysitting job is over."

Aunt Sazón drove us to Prince Griddle's for brunch. I didn't want anything because I didn't have much of an appetite, but Mom and Dad pleaded for me to eat. When the waitress came by, I ordered a single bean and cheese taco. Aunt Sazón yapped about the fun she had watching over me the last four months. She claimed I learned to cook, even though the only thing I had learned how to make was rice. She also told them I changed my wardrobe on Thanksgiving, because Lalo was my boyfriend and my attitude seemed to be doing much better. I grew furious because I realized Aunt Sazón was only happy I was finally acting like "a real girl." Mom and Dad nodded in delight, but I could tell they were confused.

"You don't want your taco?" Dad asked, noticing I had only taken a single bite.

"I'm not hungry."

"Still?" Aunt Sazón said. "You had breakfast at 8:30, you should be hungry by now."

"It's okay, sweetie," Mom said. "Don't force yourself to eat if you're not hungry."

When we got home, Mom and Dad unpacked their clothes and souvenirs. They carefully placed the new souvenirs on the compartment shelves by the fireplace. Dad pulled out a wool jacket with ARGENTINA stitched across the front.

"For you," he said.

"Thanks," I said. "But it's hot here most of the time."

"I know. This is for the days when it's not."

In the evening, Mom and Dad made four-cheese lasagna for dinner. While the lasagna baked in the oven, Dad went to the YouTube app on his phone and put on "Dance with Me" by an old band named Alphaville. He and Mom had a dance off in the kitchen and living room. I hadn't seen them dance in forever. They looked cute as they swung each other around and kissed in between their steps.

During dinner, Mom and Dad told me about their adventures, which weren't too different than their other travels. They taught. Everybody thought they were brilliant. They taught more. They researched. They ate exotic food. They taught again. For me, the most interesting tidbit was that they got to pet a llama.

"Your phone just pinged," Mom told Dad soon after dinner was over. "Do you want dessert, Elysian? I can make pudding."

"No, I'm fine," I said just Dad picked up his phone.

"Carmen! Look at this!" he exclaimed.

Mom got up and rushed over. He put his phone in her hand and when she read it, her mouth dropped wide open. "Oxford invited us?" she said. "That's phenomenal!"

"No!" I said, slamming my hands on the dining table. "You guys literally got home a few hours ago and now you're ready to leave again! All you ever do is leave me! You tell me you miss me, but the second another school gets in touch with you guys, you take off again!" I stormed off to my bedroom and locked the door behind me.

They knocked at my door softly. "*Niña*, open the door for us." I groaned out loud and let them in, but I couldn't look them in their eyes.

"What's going on?" Mom asked. "You're doing well in school, we're back home, you've got yourself a cute boyfriend, what's the problem? How's your anxiety?"

"You can talk to us," Dad said. "We're your parents."

"That's not true," I said, sitting on my bed. "I can't talk to you whenever I want. Half the time, you guys aren't home and when you are, you guys are working."

"Elysian, *niña*," Dad said. "It's hard work. It's our career."

"Yeah, I know. Forget it. Go to Oxford if you want."

"Not yet," Mom said, sitting down next to me. "Listen Elysian, Dad and I don't have to do these fellowships anymore. We can teach here on the island. Right, Marcos?"

"Of course," Dad said, nodding and tugging lightly at the end of his ponytail. "But this is *Oxford*. How about this one last fellowship, Elysian?"

"Dad," I said, dropping my head. "I knew about Oxford weeks ago."

"What? What are you talking about?" he asked with his eyes pried open. "How?"

"They sent a letter," I admitted.

"They did? When?"

"I don't remember the exact day. It was before Thanksgiving, but I shredded it."

"Elysian!" Mom said. "You shouldn't open our mail. And you definitely shouldn't be shredding it before we get the chance to see it."

"I didn't want you to know," I told them. "But I know how much Oxford means to you two. So hey... whatever. It doesn't matter."

At bedtime, I put on cozy socks to keep my feet warm and slid into bed. Dad knocked on the door just as I was falling asleep.

"Hey girlie, can I come in? How are you feeling?"

"Sleepy. But you can come in."

"Elysian, Mom and I know you have anxiety. You can talk to us about it."

"How? Nobody thinks it's real, especially this family."

"*Corazoncito*," he said, pulling up my desk chair close to my bed and gently rubbing my cheek with his hand. "Anxiety is real. I know it's real."

"How do you know?"

"My gosh, Elysian, I'm a biology professor," he said, laughing. "I have intensely studied every piece of the human body, including the brain. I'm sure."

"So, you want to put me in a hospital or something?"

"I can't decide that. What we need to do is find you a good therapist. I know a few. You're going to be okay."

"Sorry for wrecking the letter. I was just mad. Are you still going to Oxford?"

"No, I declined. Mom did too. Oxford is pure heaven for professors, but we have a piece of heaven right here at home."

"I'm not heavenly. My mind is always in hell. My name doesn't match at all."

"Your name describes you perfectly," Dad said, patting me on my forehead. "Lalo would agree."

"Lalo would be better off without me."

"He doesn't think so. Neither do I and neither does Mom. It's okay to not feel heavenly. It's completely okay. You own your emotions and no one can tell you how you should or shouldn't feel, my love."

He stood up, bent down to kiss my forehead twice, and walked out of the room quietly. I heard him say something to Mom, but couldn't make out what he said.

When I went to school the next morning, Lalo met me at the courtyard with a box of peanut butter cups. He stuck a note on top *'For you, my peanut butter.'*

"Peanut butter?" I asked.

"Ever try to stir peanut butter into a dessert? It's freaking hard. That's how tough you are."

"I feel like the weakest person ever. I'm always worrying and scared of stuff."

"And you're still going," he said. "My peanut butter."

"You ready for finals?"

"Me? Hell no, I'm doomed. I'm gonna end up taking summer school."

The school day flew by. I felt confident about all my finals except math, but I didn't feel super worried. After school, I walked with Lalo and Brandon to Emerald Beach. Since the weather was colder, there weren't as many tourists crowding the beach. Mr. Jasper stood by his storefront, ringing a bell and shouting "Half off 'til five!"

"I'm gonna get some," Brandon said. "Any of you guys want ice cream? I got enough money for all of us."

"Banana pudding," Lalo said. "How about you, Elysian?"

"Vanilla. No toppings."

"Really?" Lalo asked. "You never get vanilla."

"I wanna try it," I said with a shrug. I sat on a bench close to Jasper's and kept my eyes on Lalo and Brandon. I swore I saw another black van, but it was only my imagination. They paid for the ice creams and joined me at the bench. They were fine. No gunshots. No black vans. No blood.

"This ice cream is always amazing," Brandon said, taking another lick. "I wonder how long Mr. Jasper will have his shop. He's getting old."

"He looks around my dad's age," Lalo said. "He's got at least another twenty years of working."

"How old is your dad anyway?" Brandon asked. "Mine turned forty back in October and he's already going way downhill."

"My dad is forty-five," Lalo said. "He looks a lot better than your dad."

"My grandpa probably looks better than my dad," Brandon said. "Do you know how old your dad is, Elysian? He looks young."

"No idea. I think he's forty-five too, but I'm not sure."

After Jasper's, we walked home before the sun set. I liked the cooler weather of winter, but I hated how early it got dark. Mom was home, watching a documentary about the history of the circus. She told me dinner was in the refrigerator, and whenever I felt like eating, I could heat up the plate in the microwave for two minutes.

"I'm not hungry. Maybe later."

"How was school?"

"Okay. Where's Dad?"

"Grocery shopping. He'll be home later."

Even though I still wasn't hungry, I sat down for dinner with Mom and Dad a little after he came home. "You need to start thinking about colleges you'd like to go to," he said.

"That's easy. I'll just go to Saint Jerome since it's close."

"Don't limit yourself to Saint Jerome," Mom said. "You can go anywhere you want. Dad and I will make it happen."

"Saint Jerome is fine."

After dinner, the conversation shifted from school to therapy. Mom and Dad said they found a therapist I could visit virtually since she was located in Houston. They said she went to Harvard and completed her graduate hours at the Texas Medical Center in Houston, where she graduated at the very top of her class.

"She's one of the best in Texas," Mom said. "We're sure she can help you."

"What if she can't?" I asked.

"If you don't click with her, we'll find someone else," Dad said. "We'll do whatever you need. We promise."

On the first day of winter break, I had my first online meeting with Dr. Rafaela Trejo. She was obviously in her office as there were two large bookcases behind her and a globe on the desk beside her. Her hair was black like the night sky and curled at the ends like mine. She smiled for a minute. "Hello, Elysian."

"Hi."

"Tell me about yourself."

"Uhm," I said, hesitating. "I'm fourteen. I have a cute boyfriend named Lalo who I've known since like forever. I like history, ice cream, writing, and reading."

"Your parents mentioned you have anxiety. Would you like to tell me a little bit about your experience? What does your anxiety feel like when it's at its worst?"

I sat in silence until I thought of a proper analogy. "Have you ever been to a haunted house?" I asked her.

"I used to go back in high school. I would go again now, but with a husband and small kids, they're not exactly family friendly."

"I went to one at my school when I was in the fifth grade. It wasn't that scary, but that's what my mind feels like."

"How so?" she asked, leaning in closer to the webcam.

"You know how you have to walk through a haunted house and it's dark and you can't see well and then a ghoul or whatever jumps out at you?"

"Yes, I understand."

"The thing is those ghouls, ghosts, whatever they are, they're not real. And I know they're not real. I know they can't hurt me. But they still scare me. My mind is in this constant state of walking through a haunted house, waiting for the next thing to scare me, and I'm trying my hardest to find the exit, but I can't. I'm in an endless haunted house and I'm sick of it. I want to find the exit because I'm tired of always being scared."

"That's a wonderful example," Dr. Trejo said, smiling widely. "I understand, Elysian. I'm here to help you."

Chapter 25

On Christmas Eve, I went to the USS Defiance with Lalo. The inside was decorated with wreaths, trees, lights, and Santa Claus cutouts. We shared mozzarella sticks with marinara sauce at the Defiance Deli before we started our tour.

"Hey, how's therapy going?" he asked.

"Good, actually. We're meeting three times a week."

"Awesome. How are you feeling?"

"Better. I'm still worrying, but it's been nice to talk to someone about my fears. She just listens and doesn't tell me that I'm overreacting or that my anxiety isn't real."

"Sweet. That's exactly what you needed. Does your aunt know you're seeing a therapist? I wonder what she would have to say."

"I don't know for sure, maybe my parents told her. If she does know, I'm a hundred percent sure she thinks my parents are wasting their money to help my imaginary problem. She's an idiot."

"She is. She wants you to be someone you're not. And that's completely not cool. She needs to stick her nose in something else."

When we got to the engine room, we took a break from the tour. There were only a few people in the room with us and the engine sound effects blocked out their chatter.

"You know, I like this," Lalo said. "I like sitting here with you."

"And listening to the engines?"

"Not so much. I like your company though. Sorry if that's corny."

"It's not... observation deck?"

"Hell yeah." We waited for the other people to leave the engine room before we started our journey to the chapel. We got lucky since no one was there. Lalo scurried up the ladder and I followed behind him.

"This is such a cool spot," he said. "I'm surprised we haven't been caught yet."

"I wonder if people made out up here back in the day."

"Here? No way. Well, maybe... if they had strong enough urges."

Lalo and I looked out at Emerald Beach. The sun was bright and we heard the wind blowing against the window. The water seemed bluer and the sand glowed under the sunlight.

"You ready for Christmas?" Lalo asked. "Gladys and Octavio are cooking for us."

"It's still coming whether I'm ready or not. We go to my aunt's house every year. I'm definitely not ready for that."

"Tell Santa you want an escape for Christmas. Ready to make out?"

"I am."

He kissed me on the cheek first and then gave me a kiss on my lips. I scooted closer to him and hugged him as he put his right cheek against my left cheek. "I've been wondering," he said. "Do you ever feel anxious around me?"

"Yes, but not about you though. I worry about other stuff, but

I don't worry about you hurting me or anything. I feel safe with you. Sorry if that's corny."

"Aw," he said, blushing. "Thanks."

We stayed on the observation deck for almost an hour, kissing and looking out at Emerald Beach. For the first time since the shooting, I could look at the beach without breaking out into a sweat.

Lalo shifted himself closer to me and hugged me tightly. "Elysian," Lalo said. "You've got a great name. I love it."

"I hate it."

"I know you think it doesn't fit you. But I think it does."

"Thanks, Eduardo," I said, poking his cheek.

"Shut up," he said with a laugh, kissing me on the forehead.

Since it was cold outside, Emerald Beach was emptier, but it still looked gorgeous. It hadn't looked gorgeous to me in a long time.

Chapter 26

December 17, 2019

Dr. Trejo,

Thanks for this past year of therapy and for making me write this year-end summary. Opening up to other people is hard for me, but you've taught me how to make it a little easier.

A lot has changed. Nate moved away to a place called Bat Springs, Texas. His parents split and he chose to live with his dad instead of his mom. Lalo told me there's a good restaurant there called El Paso Paradise. He ate there with his parents and Gladys when they went on vacation this past summer.

Tiana and me are closer friends now. Twice a week, I help her parents at their bakery. I've learned how to bake loads of desserts. It's been a neat experience and her parents pay me ten bucks an hour. I should've given Tiana a chance sooner. She's a lot nicer than I thought.

The Emerald Beach Shooter and Gladys' kidnappers were finally caught. They were Octavio's old friends. Turns out Octavio had a big life insurance policy on Gladys and he asked his friends to kill her and make it look like an accident, but they screwed up the plan.

Octavio had been cheating on Gladys for a while and wanted the money to start a new life with the other woman. Mr. Meyer overheard Octavio talking about it at Isle of Darkness, even with the club music playing. He immediately put Octavio in a headlock and beat on him until the cops showed up. Mr. Meyer got a medal of honor from Patricia Montoya, the mayor of Rey Carlos Island. He's also lost a lot of weight and doesn't drink or smoke anymore. He starts night school for his GED in January. And, he's started going to synagogue services again. Even Brandon can't solve that mystery.

I'm relieved to know Octavio and his friends are in prison. And as for the Emerald Beach Shooting, it was Octavio. He did the shooting while his buddies kidnapped Gladys. Now that the search is over, there aren't as many cop cars driving around Rey Carlos like before. My city feels safe again. Gladys has a new boyfriend, too. She's dating Officer Shawn Riley, the cop who rescued her from her torture chamber inside the USS Defiance.

My parents are teaching less now. They still work full time, but they've stopped making presentations and doing endless research. They also haven't traveled this year. When I get home from school, they're home within an hour. I don't see or talk to my aunt and her family as much as before. They gave me the nickname "Nutcase" when they found out I was seeing you, so I couldn't keep being around them. You've taught me my mental health is what is most important.

I'm doing well in high school. Brandon and Lalo are, too. Brandon's mom recently moved back to Rey Carlos Island, so he gets to see her more often. The other day, he mentioned his dad's parents are coming to visit for a couple of weeks. He's excited to meet his grandparents for the first time. In fact, he's so excited, he's been watching lots of Judaism documentaries instead of murder ones, so he can talk to them about something they like.

Lalo and I are doing fantastic. He's seen me have panic and anxiety attacks throughout this whole year, but he stays close to me until the attacks end. When they're over, he kisses me on my cheek or my forehead and tells me three things he likes about me. I don't know if I'm in love yet, but if I ever do fall in love, it'll definitely be with Lalo.

I want to say thanks again for helping me out. Sometimes I still feel like I'm in a haunted house, but not as much anymore. I feel better. I willingly go to Emerald Beach with my friends once a week. A year and a half ago, there was no way I could have done that.

I'm not exactly there yet, but I'm starting to feel like my name fits me. I read about the Elysian Fields in one of Mom's books. It said the Greeks believed the Elysian Fields was a place where heroes would go, heroes everybody looked up to, including strong heroes like Heracles. I told Lalo I don't deserve to have the name Elysian because I'm nobody's hero. He told me I was wrong. He said I am a hero to myself. He said I've been walking through a haunted house for a long time and I face my fears full force, every single day, 365 days a year. So, I guess I am a hero.

I'm excited about our second year of therapy. Thanks for everything. One day, when I'm feeling much better, Heaven might be me.

-*Elysian Lecaro*

Mental Health Resources For Adolescents and Young Adults

Powered by the Society for Adolescent Health and Medicine

YOUTH FRIENDLY MENTAL HEALTH ONLINE RESOURCES

- **Center for Young Women's Health and Young Men's Health**: These websites provides a series of guides on emotional health, including on test anxiety, depression, bullying, and eating disorders (www.youngwomenshealth.org) and (www.youngmenshealthsite.org)
- **Go Ask Alice!**: Geared at young adults, this question and answer website contains a large database of questions about a variety of concerns surrounding emotional health (www.goaskalice.columbia.edu)
- **Girls Health.Gov**: The "Your Feelings" section of this website offers guidance to teenage girls on recognizing a mental health problem, getting help, and talking to parents (http://girlshealth.gov/feelings/index.html)
- **Jed Foundation**: Promoting emotional health and prevent suicide among college students, this website provides an online resource center, **ULifeline**, a public dialogue forum,

Half of Us, and **Transition Year**, resources and tools to help students transition to college (http://www.jedfoundation.org/students)

- **Kelty Mental Health Resource Center**: Reference sheets are provided that list top websites, books, videos, toolkits and support for mental health disorders (http://keltymentalhealth.ca/youth-and-young-adults)
- **Reach Out**: This website provides information on specific mental health disorders, as well as resources to help teens make safe plans when feeling suicidal, and helpful tips on how to relax (http://au.reachout.com/)
- **Teens Health:** Providing a safe place for teens who need honest and accurate information, this website provides resources on mental health issues (http://teenshealth.org/teen/your_mind/)
- **Teen Mental Health:** Geared towards teenagers, this website provides learning tools on a variety of mental illnesses, videos, and resources for friends (http://teenmentalhealth.org/)

APPS AND TECH SERVICES

- **Beacon 2.0**: Beacon is a portal to online applications (websites, mobile applications and internet support groups) for mental disorders reviewed and rated by health experts (https://beacon.anu.edu.au/)
- **Health Talk:** This website reflects the lived experience of mental health conditions, including research-based modules with hours of recording and analysis (

www.healthtalk.org/peoples-experiences/mental-health)
- **Mindfulness for Teens:** This website has resources to help teens use mindfulness to handle stress and includes apps to practice meditation and guided mediation recordings (http://mindfulnessforteens.com/)
- **Mood 247**: A text messaging system that provides an easy way to record how you're feeling and tracks your daily moods to share with friends, family, or a health professional (https://www.mood247.com/)
- **Strength of Us:** An online community designed to inspire young adults impacted by mental health issues to think positive, stay strong and achieve goals through peer support and resource sharing (http://strengthofus.org/)

MENTAL HEALTH RESOURCES INSTITUTES

- **American Academy of Child and Adolescent Psychiatry**: This resource center includes videos, ways to get help, and advocacy campaigns (www.aacap.org/AACAP/Families_and_Youth/Youth_Resources/Home.aspx)
- **National Alliance on Mental Health**: Find resources for youth, including information on managing your mental health in college and making friends (www.nami.org/Find-Support/Teens-and-Young-Adults)
- **National Institute of Mental Health**: This website provides easy-to read guides and brochures to help better understand a variety of mental health disorders (www.nimh.nih.gov/health/index.shtml)
- **Substance Abuse and Mental Health Services Adminis-**

tration: SAMHSA provides information on mental health services and treatment centers through a service locator (https://findtreatment.samhsa.gov/)

MENTAL HEALTH MEDICATION GUIDES

- **Head Meds:** This website gives young people focused information about the most common medicines prescribed for mental health conditions (http://www.headmeds.org.uk/)
- **Making Healthy Choices:** This guide provides information for youth in foster care related to making decisions about their mental health, treatment options, and the use of psychotropic medications (www.childwelfare.gov/pubs/-makinghealthychoices/)

HELPLINES

- **Campaign Against Living Miserably (CALM)**: Visit (www.thecalmzone.net) or UK residents call 0800-58-58-58
- **Crisis Text Line:** Visit (www.crisistextline.org/) or Text "START" to 741-741
- **Lifeline Crisis Chat:** Visit (www.crisischat.org/) to chat with crisis centers around the U.S.
- **List of International Suicide Hotlines:** Visit (www.suicide.org/international-suicide-hotlines.html)
- **Love is Respect:** Visit (www.loveisrespect.org/), text "LOVEIS" to 22522, or call 1-866-331-9474 to talk with a

peer advocate to prevent and end abusive relationships
- **National Eating Disorder Association:** Visit (www.nationaleatingdisorders.org/) or call 1-800-931-2237
- **National Suicide Prevention Lifeline:** Visit (www.suicidepreventionlifeline.org/) or call 1-800-273-TALK (8255)

ADVOCACY

- **Active Minds:** The leading nonprofit that empowers college students to speak openly about mental health, Active Minds aims to educate others and encourage help-seeking (http://activeminds.org/)
- **Gay, Lesbian & Straight Education Network:** GLSEN is the leading national education organization focused on ensuring safe schools for all students. This website provides resources on finding GSA Chapters, and tools on how to establish or re-establish a GSA (http://www.glsen.org/)
- **StopBullying.Gov**: This website offers resources specifically for teens to prevent bullying in their schools and communities and provides resources for those being bullied (http://www.stopbullying.gov/)
- **Teens Against Bullying**: Created by and for teens, this website is a place for middle and high school students to find ways to address bullying, take action, be heard, and own an important social cause (http://www.pacerteensagainstbullying.org/)
- **Time to Change**: As England's biggest program to challenge mental health stigma and discrimination, this advocacy website provides ways to join the campaign and get others

involved (www.time-to-change.org.uk/)
- **Youth Resource**: Created by and for LGBTQ young people, this website provides information and resources on self-harm and suicide, personal stories and accounts, and useful hotlines (www.youthresource.com/)

Dear Young Reader

Do you ever feel like Elysian? Do you ever feel like you're walking through a haunted house and you can't find the exit, no matter how hard you try? Do you ever feel like nobody loves you and no one would care if you weren't around?

These feelings are very common. You are not alone in your emotions. How do I know this? When I was your age, I had these feelings and sometimes, I still do. There's an idea that depression and anxiety can't be seen like physical illnesses, but that's not quite true. The signs are pretty clear: feeling down, no interest in former hobbies, suicidal thoughts, irrational fears, panic attacks, hyperventilating, etc. We CAN see these illnesses – we just choose to ignore them.

Life can be tough – you know that without a doubt. School is hectic with everything you need to learn, drama with friends, romances, working a job, preparing for college – all these things lead to major STRESS! Stress can be a trigger for depression and anxiety, but doctors don't know for sure what causes depression and anxiety in each person. Whatever the cause is, remember something very important:

IT IS OKAY TO FEEL THE WAY YOU FEEL.

People in your life might tell you that you have no reason to feel depressed or you have no reason to be anxious. Hearing this only makes you feel worse and this idea is ridiculous. Imagine the last time you had a cold. Remember the sneezing, the coughing, the fever, the stuffy mucus in your nose? What did you do? You probably went to see a doctor, or you took some cold medication and then you felt better. Can you imagine having a cold and someone looks at you blowing your nose and tells you, "Excuse me, you have no reason to have a cold! Get over it!" How silly would that sound? Likewise, when you are not feeling okay emotionally, it is totally acceptable to seek help just as you would for a cold.

You might be thinking, "Okay, Ms. Campos, thanks for the lecture, but where on earth do I get help for how I'm feeling?" Great question! The Vital Narrative Press team and I have put together a list of resources for you to check out. We encourage you to try them and decide which one works best for you. If you need more resources, you can talk to your school counselor or ask a trusted adult, whether that person is a teacher, a parent, a mentor, clergyperson, just anyone you feel most comfortable with, and see what else you can find.

Lastly, if you are having suicidal thoughts, seek help immediately. You are loved. You are wanted. You are important. You might not feel like you are, but trust me, you are someone's priceless treasure. Nobody in the whole world has your same DNA or your same fingerprints. That's how unique you are – you are very special.

Never forget that.

About the Author

Darlene P. Campos earned her MFA in Creative Writing from the University of Texas at El Paso. She also graduated from the University of Houston with a BA in English–Creative Writing and a minor in Medicine and Social Studies. She is from Guayaquil, Ecuador, but currently lives in Houston, TX with her husband David and an adorable pet rabbit named Jake. Her website is www.darlenepcampos.com *(photo by Splantaneous Photography)*

You can connect with me on:
- http://darlenepcampos.com
- https://twitter.com/DarleneCampos91
- https://www.facebook.com/DarlenePCampos

Also by Darlene P. Campos

Summer Camp Is Cancelled

http://bit.ly/SummerCampIsCancelled

238 pp.   11-year-old Lyndon, the son of Mexican immigrants, is secretly in love with his best friend Melody, a deaf girl who uses her white board to communicate. When his plans to spend the summer at an exclusive camp with Melody are thwarted, Lyndon is forced to spend his vacation waiting for her to return home while working in his family's restaurant, aggravating his devout Catholic grandmother and avoiding his annoying Uncle Manny.

Behind Mount Rushmore

http://bit.ly/BehindMountRushmore

234 pp. *Behind Mount Rushmore* is a coming-of-age young adult novel about Nimo Thunderclap, a young man who grows up on Pine Ridge Indian Reservation in South Dakota.